Best wishes

B Holmes

CW00457719

Jake's Women

Jake Bridger left a string of broken women behind him – like a kid dropping litter on the boardwalk. He used them, one by one, and then dumped them. The upshot was that there were three young, vulnerable girls left to fend for themselves in the dangerous wilderness that was the frontier of the Old West. He thought nothing more about them.

But what he didn't know was that there was a fourth girl. One, not so young, not so vulnerable, and one with vengeance in her heart....

Jake's Women

B. J. Holmes

A Black Horse Western

ROBERT HALE · LONDON

ISBN 0 7090 7179 5

Robert Hale Limited
Clerkenwell House
Clerkenwell Green
London EC1R 0HT

Für Renate

Typeset by
Derek Doyle & Associates, Liverpool.
Printed and bound in Great Britain by
Antony Rowe Limited, Wiltshire

1

Trying to fill inside straights is a sucker's game. That's what the bozo the other side of the table had tried to do. So when the schmuck tried it a third time, Jake knew he had a goose ready for plucking.

And some goose. It wasn't just the tailored suit and gold cufflinks that said the guy was used to swanning into classy city restaurants where they knew his name. It was the stack of bills on the table in front of the shiny cufflinks – not to mention the fat wallet they came out of.

So Jake took the bit between his teeth and began to raise the ante – up, up, till the stakes became too heavy for the regulars, run-of-the-mill cowpokes with no more than loose change in their pockets. After a couple of high-rolling hands the Fat Goose and Jake were the only ones left in the game.

All went well until the bird said, 'Well, sir, that's enough for me.' He was looking blankly at Jake's three kings. And the monarchs, equally devoid of expression, were staring blankly right back at the poor fellow. 'Run of the cards just don't seem to be

5

working my way,' he went on, pushing the pot in Jake's direction with palms exaggeratedly flattened out to signify a finality to the proceedings. 'I thank you for the game, sir,'

'Are you sure?' Jake said, leaning forward to claim his winnings. One of the hands that drew in the money was shy of a little finger. But lack of a digit was no hindrance in its present task of gathering in bills and coins. Just as earlier it had been no handicap in the sleight of hand necessary to position cards to the advantage of its owner. Scooping the money, he weighed it in his hand. 'Are you sure?' he repeated. 'While you still got some chance of getting this back?' The man shook his head. 'The way my luck's panning out tonight I think that chance is remote.'

'Well, I thank you for the game, sir,' Jake echoed. He didn't want to push it. The ending had come so abruptly he had a feeling the guy suspected he had slipped the last king.

He watched the man rise and head for the bar, then followed him. He had rooked the guy of a hundred dollars which was a good night's work; but for a man like Jake that was not enough when he knew there was more. A lot more. A thirsty man doesn't leave a well after one sip.

'At least allow me to buy you a drink,' he said when he had joined the man.

'What's the difference?' the guy chuckled drily. 'I buy, it's my money. You buy, it's still my money. Don't take offence, sir, but it's one of my rules to buy my own liquor.'

Now Jake was sure the fellow had seen him grift with that last king. Maybe the fellow couldn't prove it, maybe he didn't want to cause a ruckus, maybe he couldn't handle the physicality of a ruckus. For whatever reason, it wasn't worth Jake's while pushing his own luck. 'I understand, sir. No offence took. I bid you goodnight.' And he left the saloon.

Back in his hotel room he paced the floor. Fran was reading a book.

'You might be interested in this,' she said. 'By Charles Dickens. It's about an old crook called Fagin who took young kids and taught them how to be crooks. Might ring a few bells.'

'Listen,' he said, without hearing. 'Put that damn book down. Business calls. Found us a mark. Over in the Crescent Hotel yonder. Guy's loaded but I figure he's onto me so he ain't gonna let me get close again. Here's what we do . . . .'

Half an hour later he was standing at the window while Fran was sitting on the bed, a bulging valise beside her.

'Right, the stage's jes' rolled in,' he observed. His plan was to make it appear that she had only just arrived.

She had changed into a different dress and coat, ones she had not worn since their arrival two days ago. She'd reshaped her hair. And to make sure, she wore a semi-veiled hat.

'OK, do your stuff, gal.'

Minutes later she entered The Crescent Hotel

and asked for a room. On the way to the stairs she
espied the man Jake had described ensconced at
the back of the saloon. Once alone in her room,
she looked out of the window to re-establish a link
with Jake. She could make out his figure in the
darkness leaning against a stanchion on the
boardwalk opposite. He lit a cigarette, his signal
of acknowledgement. Then she moved the lamp
across the window, the first of two signals she was
to give.

Downstairs, in the restaurant section away
from the main drinking area, she took a meal in
keeping with her role as a weary traveller newly
arrived in town. When she had finished she took
her coffee into the saloon and sat at a table adja-
cent to the man, keeping her back to the other
patrons. She paid no attention to him but could
already feel his eyes upon her. Act like you're
minding your own business, Jake had said. After
a while she took a cigarette from her bag and
pretended to look in vain for matches, then leaned
over and asked the fellow for a light.

'Sorry, ma'am, don't smoke,' he said, 'but I can
sure get you a light.' He went to the bar and
bought a box of matches. Returning, he lit her
cigarette then handed her the box.

'Thank you,' she said, trying not to cough at the
biting unfamiliarity of smoke in her mouth. She
made to take out her purse. 'How much do I owe
you?'

'No, no. Don't mention it, ma'am. Compliments
of Herbert Fisher.' He stood awkwardly before her

for a moment, then asked, 'May I join you, ma'am?'

'I'm afraid I won't be very good company.' Be aloof, Jake had said. She half-smiled, sighed and added, 'I haven't yet gotten over being bounced all over the place in what goes for transport in this part of the world.'

Undeterred, he took a seat beside her. 'How far have you travelled?'

'Far enough.'

'I mean where from?'

'You ask your questions in a forthright manner, sir.' Don't give anything away had been Jake's instruction.

'I apologize, ma'am. Simply making conversation is all. It's just that I'm a guest at the hotel too, and I figure we're the only two partaking of the accommodation facilities.' He threw a disdainful glance around the room, the work-grimed cowboys. 'Not the most salubrious of places. I can tell that a lady such as yourself must have stayed in better.'

Due to the fact that she was a simple girl from a poor homestead the observation would not ordinarily have been true. But then she had found herself in the company of Jake and pricey accommodation often went with the job.

'Yes,' she said. 'I've noticed the place doesn't exactly run to bell-boys. Still, can't complain. Not much to choose out here.'

'And what brings you – out here?'

She tried to look nonchalant in her handling of

the evil smelling smoke as she said, 'There you go again.'

'Excuse me, ma'am. I guess I do ask too many questions. Just my nature.' He watched her finish her coffee. 'Say, can I buy you a proper drink, ma'am, to kinda make amends?'

'I'm afraid I don't take alcohol.'

He paused, then said, 'The name's Herbert K. Fisher. Call me Bert.'

She smiled slightly as a sign of acquiescence. 'Eleanor Vanderberg. Pleased to make your acquaintance.' That was the society-style name Jake had suggested.

'Eleanor? A distinguished name.'

'Distinguished? I've not heard that one before. I must say your approach is different.'

'You misunderstand me, ma'am. I'm not making an approach, merely commenting honestly on the regality of your name.'

'Regality?'

'Yes. Eleanor was one of the queens of England. The dearly beloved wife of Edward the First. You know, so enamoured of her was he, that when she died he set up crosses to her memory across the length and breadth of the land.'

She nodded, then said, 'I doubt if they called her Ellie.'

'I'm sure they did. Is what they call you? My, my. Ellie is real feminine, ma'am.'

She looked around the room, shaking her head. 'Queen, eh? Well, this sure is some place for a queen to spend her birthday.' She made the statement in a low voice as though not for his ears.

'What was that you say? Birthday?'

'No matter,' she said. 'Just talking to myself.'

'Birthday, eh? This calls for a celebration. Champagne.' He went to the bar, exchanged a few words with the bartender and eventually came back with a bottle and a couple of glasses. 'As one might have expected. No bell-boys, no champagne. All they have is this wine. Domestic at that. But better than nothing. Never mind that business of no alcohol, this is a special occasion, my dear.'

'I shouldn't have mentioned it. Listen, I'm very tired and it's very kind of you but I really must rest.'

'Ellie, you can't celebrate your birthday alone in a strange town. And I have bought the wine in your honour.'

She deliberately procrastinated, pretending to mull the matter over, then said, 'I am ready to drop. I have to lie down. The only thing I can suggest is that you come to my room for a short while and I'll share a drink with you there, seeing as you've gone to the expense and all.'

It was sometime later in the semi-darkness of the upstairs room. Fran lay on the bed with her shoes off while the man was sitting in a chair beside her. An oil-lamp glowed low on a table. They had shared a few glasses and she had pretended to be getting dozy, allowing the man to do all the talking.

'My, it's getting so hot in here,' she said after a

while. 'It must be the wine, I told you I'm not used to drinking.' Her dress was already unbuttoned a little at the top. Eyes half closed, she undid buttons down to her waist exposing the bulge of her breasts above her chemise. The light from the side cast shadows that emphasized their roundness.

'Have another drink,' he said, 'there's still a lot left.'

'I shouldn't.'

He refilled her glass and helped her onto her elbow so she could take a few sips. She lowered her head and closed her eyes. Returning the glass to the table he sat beside her on the bed and held her hand. 'You sure are a goddess,' he whispered. 'A Greek goddess.'

He began to stroke her arm. 'I've never seen such beauty.'

Bending over he kissed her neck tentatively. Meeting no rebuke, his lips slowly moved down her throat and he began to groan when they met the thrust of soft round flesh. Her arms rose around him as his face plunged between her breasts. Then she started wrenching at his shirt, pulling it up from the back, her fingers kneading the flesh of his back.

'Hey, slow down, big boy' she whispered. 'You don't have to go like an express train.' She found the whole thing repulsive but she had a role to play. Failure would mean a beating by Jake.

For a few moments she allowed him to grope and grunt, then she murmured, 'Take off your clothes. It's better that way.'

'You've done this before.'

She stiffened. 'I'm not a whore, Mr Fisher.'
There was a deliberate hint of reprimand in her
voice. She had him on a hook and had to slow him
down, play him like a fish on a line.

'Forgive me, I intended no slight.' He took his
weight off her and began wrenching at his
trousers.

Now free to move she rose from the bed. 'Uh,
am I thirsty.'

'I'll get you some more wine.'

'No, I feel like some water,' she said.

'I'll get it, ma'am.'

'No, you finish getting those duds off. It's been
a long time since I've seen a man's body.' She
picked up the lamp and passed it across the
window as she moved towards the water jar.

Outside, the planking creaked as Jake shifted
his weight. How long was she going to be? Then he
saw the signal and the planking creaked one final
time as he left the boardwalk.

Minutes later the couple were back on the bed
and she was feeling eager hands once more
exploring her body. Over the man's shoulder all
she could see was the ceiling. Wisps of cobwebs
threw their own exotic shadows. She gnawed the
inside of her cheek uneasily. Despite the man's
observation this kind of thing was still new to her.
Everything she had done and said had been on
Jake's instruction. Jake had been the only one to
use her body in this way. He was good-looking and
at first she had succumbed to his charm. But she

soon learned that he was short-tempered and cruel.

'Say, you ever done it like dogs do it?' the man whispered.

She didn't answer right away. Her mind was on Jake. Had he seen the signal? How long was he going to be? Then, 'I haven't done it much at all, Mr Fisher. What do you mean?'

He chuckled. 'You know like dogs in the street. You must have seen 'em. Always time to learn new tricks. I'll teach you. Turn that gorgeous body over and shuffle down the bed.'

She took her time complying. Where was Jake? 'Like this you mean?'

'No, come down lower.'

She eased down further.

'Now open your legs.'

He'd just gripped her hips when the door burst open.

'So this is what you get up to!'

The man turned to see a figure framed in the light of the corridor, gun in hand. 'What the . . . ?'

The man closed the door. 'Don't move, you bastard,' he said, keeping the gun levelled as he crossed the room and turned up the lamp.

He took in the scene and advanced towards the man. 'What burn-in hell depravities has this gutter-rat been forcing you to do, honey?'

The man backed a step, his hands over his now inactive private parts. 'Ain't forced myself on anybody, mister. She was a willing party.' He'd barely had a chance to finish speaking before

Jake whopped him across the head with the gun, felling him.

'Willing party! Don't you dare blacken the name of my woman like that.'

A blanket now draped around her, Fran stood beside Jake who put a protective arm around her. 'You're safe now, honey. Get dressed.'

Still on the floor, the man scrabbled backwards but Jake followed, looming over him. 'Take advantage of a poor woman, would you? I've chased my wife over half the county, then I find her in the clutches of a depraved bastard like you.'

'Your wife?'

'Yeah. We had a slight difference of opinion, is all, and she lit out. I know your type, feller. Taking advantage of a poor female in a distressed state.'

'I had no idea, mister.'

'You know what the penalty is in this county for abusing a man's wife?'

'No, I'm not from these parts. Just a drummer passing through.'

'Well, we protect our women in these parts. A five hundred dollar fine. That is, after a whipping from me.'

Fear contorted the man's features. 'Don't hit me again, mister. I didn't mean no harm. Just a lonely man looking for a bit of company.'

'And a hefty prison term,' Jake went on. 'Me and the county judge are pals. Went to school together. Between the two of us we'll make sure you don't see daylight for quite a spell.'

The man was shaking a lowered head. 'That'd ruin my business.'

'And your name in the papers,' Jake continued. 'That would dirty up customer relations for a hundred miles or more.' He glanced at Fran. 'When you're dressed, honey, go and fetch the sheriff.'

The man leaned over and took the discarded blanket to cover his lower parts. 'Listen, mister, I can pay.'

'You're darn right you'll pay. In court first thing in the morning.'

'No, I mean I can pay you. I've been doing well lately. Get my wallet. It's in my jacket. You can have it all if we can come to some arrangement.'

They rode for two hours before they pulled in to bivouac. It had been a clear moonlit night so the going had been easy. With their blankets prepared for sleep, they were sitting beside a small fire, taking a last drink.

'The knucklehead wasn't kidding when he said he'd been doing well,' Jake reflected, looking at the bills in his hand that he had just counted. 'Over four hundred bucks. And his ring and cufflinks will fetch a nice piece of change too.'

'Now you've got a fat bankroll, does that mean we're not going to bother with the Carver City job?'

'Hell, no. This is chicken-feed compared to what we'll get out of the bank. 'Sides, I put a lot of effort into planning Carver City.' He flourished the wad.

'But grab it where and when you can is my motto.' He stashed the money back in his jacket. 'A good night's work there, honey. You played your part well.'

She finished her coffee and upended the dregs in the fire. 'Must say, that was very kind of you to leave the feller a few dollars.'

'Kindness don't come into it, gal. I left him just enough dough to pay his hotel bill and scuttle out of town. That's all he wants to do now. Get the business behind him and never hear of it again. See, a well-heeled guy who can't pay his hotel bill would attract attention. Like the law, mebbe. Then somebody might start asking the kind of questions that haven't occurred to him.' He touched his forehead and winked. 'Method in madness.'

He flicked the butt of his cigarette into the fire, chuckling as he did so. 'That was some scene I broke in on – you with your bare ass stuck out like that.' He mused on the image and added, 'That horseplay back there must have turned you on, baby. And as far as I could see it wasn't finished. I can finish it off for you.'

'No, Jake, he didn't turn me on. Fact is, I couldn't wait for you to come busting through that door so I'd get those pawing hands off me.'

He mused further, recalling the tableau that had met his eyes in the hotel room. 'Well, gal, it sure turned me on. Come here.' And he pulled her to him.

She closed her eyes and let things happen.

2

Bad days can start off like any other with no warning of what's coming. That's the way it was that morning in Carver City. The sun was shining, genteel bonneted women moved from store to store and kids were playing in the alleys. Barkeeps brushed dust from the boardwalks outside the saloons.

From the window of the County and Plains Bank, Nehemiah Stein looked out on the bustling scene. Yeah, looked like a good day. And tomorrow was going to be even better. In his pocket was a wire informing him that the biggest herd the town had ever seen was headed their way and that the outfit's boss had the notion to do his transacting through the County and Plains. It had been weeks since Stein had received the message. That had given him enough time to notify head office to send extra funds. Duly a strongbox had come in via the railroad and the greenbacks it contained were now packing his safe. That very morning an outrider had brought the news that the herd was but ten miles away. It would be bedded down that evening, then tomorrow the marketing would start. A couple of wealthy-looking buyers had already arrived in town and were now ensconced in the hotel. Big money would go, big money would come back – and there would be hefty percentages for the bank.

He exhaled noisily in satisfaction and turned from the window to look at the customers coming and going. Yes sirree, it was boom time in Carver City. Even better, there seemed no end to the upward rise in prosperity. OK, some day the railroad would push further west, taking the railhead with it; new cattle trails would be forged. But for the time being seemed like nothing could break the high roll. He crossed the lobby and passed through the hinged section of the counter. At the rear he strode up and down overseeing the tellers at their work. There were already three on the payroll and that set him to pondering. If things continued on the up and up he would have to indent for more staff. More staff meant more responsibility, and from that followed plain justification for his pressing head office for a raise.

In his office he sat down and ran his fingers admiringly over the veneer of his desk. Then he lit a cigar and opened up a ledger. Meanwhile outside, a young woman paused to allow a wagon to pass, then made her way across the street. At the other side she raised her long bustled dress, just enough to give her dainty feet clearance in stepping onto the boardwalk. Once on the planking she faltered a little. The wings of her bonnet largely hid her face but from her posture an observer might have concluded she looked unwell. But no passer-by gave her a glance. She made for the entrance to the bank and a man coming out held the door for her.

Inside, she studied the queue leading to a teller's grill, but instead of joining it she stepped back and leaned against the wall, as though things were becoming too much for her. Her head slumped forward, she stood there for a moment, then gradually slid down the wall. A few seconds passed before anyone saw her. An old lady concluded her business and put her withdrawn bills into her purse.

'Oh, what's the matter, dear?' she asked as she turned from the counter and saw the crumpled figure. She moved quickly forward and knelt beside the younger one. She made a quick appraisal, then looked up. 'Can someone get a glass of water?'

A clerk looked quizzically from the counter then put a TILL CLOSED notice against his grille. As he disappeared into the back, a tall elegantly dressed man carrying a small case broke from the queue.

'Let me see, ma'am,' he said. 'I'm a doctor.'

By the time Stein arrived with a teller bearing a glass of water, the man had made his own appraisal.

'You the manager?'

'Yes, sir. Stein's the name.'

'Well, Mr Stein, the young lady plainly needs a rest and I would like to examine her a little more closely. Is there somewhere private we can take her?'

'Certainly, my room in back.'

The two men helped the staggering girl through the building and laid her on a couch in the manager's office, her eyes closed.

The dark-suited man took off her bonnet, revealing a blotchy face. 'Doesn't look good,' he said.

'What's the matter with her?' Stein asked.

'Not sure yet.' The man felt the pulse, then examined her throat. He looked at her arms, the back of her neck. He smelled her breath and pulled a wry face. 'Mr Stein, you have a real problem here. In fact your town's got a problem. This girl's got the pox.'

Stein's face whitened. 'Smallpox?'

'The very same.'

'You sure?'

'Seen enough of it in my time.'

The bank manager pulled out a handkerchief, mopped his brow then dropped into a chair repeating the word 'God' over and over in a low voice. The other was standing erect, a new seriousness permeating his face, posture and voice.

'The whole town's got to be quarantined. Nobody must enter or leave.'

The manager wiped the back of his neck with the handkerchief. 'You don't understand, Doctor. We got big business tomorrow. The biggest herd that's ever hit town. There's marketing to be done. And the catering for the trail hands. That'll bring in a fortune to the saloons and stores.'

The other shook his head. 'I'm sorry, Mr Stein. The town can say *adios* to all that.'

'You sure that's smallpox? I think we should have a second opinion on this.'

'I've told you, this is smallpox all right. But I agree about getting your local sawbones in. Go tell one of your clerks to fetch him.' He gestured a thumb to the door. 'The sooner he knows about this better. I'm a stranger here. I can help out a spell but it'll be his job to organize things, arrange the quarantine. And to notify the state authorities, of course, as he's legally required to do.'

Stein made to move but fell back. When he did rise, he crossed the room and closed the door. 'Listen, is there some other way we can handle this, Doc? Quarantining the place, that'll kill the town. We're talking about folk's livelihoods here.'

The other grunted cynically. 'Kill the town? That's an appropriate metaphor. We're talking pox here, mister. There's likely to be a lot of dying as it is.'

Stein looked at the girl, careful to maintain a safe distance. 'She can't stay here.'

'You know her?'

'Never seen her before.'

'So you don't know if she has folks in town?'

'No.'

The manager thought about it. 'She's a stranger all right. Until we know otherwise I think we should assume she's by herself.'

'Not a good assumption, Mr Stein. All her contacts have to be identified.'

Stein exhaled noisily, marking his frustration. 'No, no. She's gotta be took some place. Quick as possible. Out of the way. Out of town if possible.'

'That's right. Somewhere completely isolated.'

'And the less said about this the better. It'd start a panic. There must be some way round the business.'

The doctor edged his backside onto the desk. 'Mind, suppose something could be arranged. As she's gotta be moved anyhows. Now, I might be amenable to helping you out of the problem. I'm a doctor with ethics, but I'm also a man of the world. Trouble is, if I'm any judge, the poor gal ain't gonna live long enough to pay my bill.'

Stein raised his hands. 'I can pay that.'

The doctor thought on the matter. 'Listen, if I'm thinking what you're thinking, that is, me taking her a real long ways away, and saying nothing, we're talking big potatoes. If I'm gonna compromise my principles, it's gotta be worth my while.'

'How big?'

'A grand. For any inconvenience, you understand. Not to mention the risk I'm taking of catching the disease.'

'A grand'll be no problem. I can pay you from bank funds. Once I've explained the situation to my fellow trustees, they'll sanction the payment. I know it. A thing like this would gravely damage bank profits.'

The man thought more on it. 'OK. But I'll need a buggy. A surrey, something civilized. Not a rough plank buckboard. We got a stretch of travelling to do if you want her well clear of your little town.'

'You can have mine. It can be here in minutes.'

'OK. Tell your clerk to fetch it and draw it up out back. And tell them to fetch one or two big blankets. I leave it to your discretion whether you tell them about the smallpox.'

'I think it better they don't know,' the manager said. 'I'll think of something to tell them.'

'Just make sure I get an unimpeded exit out of town with the poor gal. It's in the interests of you and everybody else in your precious burg that nobody gets too close to the gal. And there's no guarantee on this. The thing might be spreading already. You understand that?'

The manager nodded. 'I'll make sure that nobody stops you.' With that he disappeared through the door. Shortly, wheels and horse's hoofs could be heard.

'It's all ready,' Stein said, entering from the back bearing some neatly folded blankets.

'OK,' the man said. 'I suggest you give your clerks the morning off. Then lock all the doors. We don't want anybody stumbling in until we've got the girl out. You got some kind of TEMPORARILY CLOSED notice?'

'Yes.'

'Put that on the front door.'

Stein did as he was bid.

'OK,' the other said when the manager returned, 'everybody gone?'

'Yes.'

'OK, get the cash we agreed on while I wrap the gal up.'

Stein hastened to the strongroom so quickly he didn't notice the other ignore the girl and kneel down to his leather case and open it. Inside his office the manager fiddled at the safe door till it swung open. He turned to speak but no words came from his mouth – just a grunt as the butt of a Colt single-action .45 slammed down on the back of his head.

He slumped to the floor with no more interest in matters medical, financial or otherwise.

'OK, Fran,' the man said loudly as he sheathed his gun. 'You can stir yourself now and come and give me a hand to tie this bozo up.'

The girl appeared at the door, all signs of illness gone, save for the blotchy make-up on her face. 'So far so good, Jake,' she said.

The man grinned at her. 'The way you act, Fran, if ever you wanna go on the stage, them fancy actresses will have real competition.' There was a chair in the corner and they heaved the corpulent bank manager into it. Jake took a length of rope from his bag and securely tied the man in place, fixing a gag hard round his mouth to complete the exercise.

Only when he was sure there would be no movement or sound from the man did he return to the safe. He stood before it, assessing the take.

'Just as I calculated. The thing is fuller than a squirrel's winter hidy-hole.'

'You sure know how to plan things, Jake.'

'That's right. And the word is "plan". Only a bonehead busts through a bank door with guns in his hand, hoping there's a good pull in the box. Now see if you can find some big bags. There must be some about the place.'

Some fifteen minutes later they were seated in the surrey, its boot weighed down. For appearances' sake the girl lay slumped at Jake's side, one of the blankets around her. Stein was locked in his own strongroom and a notice was in place on the front door. All doors were locked and nobody had seen them load up. The man called Jake put on a doleful face and flicked the reins. As he pulled out onto the main drag some people looked. They knew something was going on, but whatever it was it had been sanctioned by Stein so it had to be above board. They whispered amongst themselves but were content in the knowledge that the full explanation would materialize. Only one person bothered to keep his eyes on the surrey as it blurred into the distance: an old guy seated on a boardwalk chair at the end of town. An old guy with nothing better to do. When the surrey had disappeared completely, he returned to smoking his pipe and contemplating whatever men in such circumstances contemplate, giving no further mind to the vanished object.

Way out of sight of the town, Jake turned off the trail and headed the surrey into the cover of trees where two hidden horses were standing patiently. They changed into trail clothes and transferred the money to plain-looking saddle-bags. The girl cleaned her face, they mounted up and headed across country.

Back in Carver City it was three hours later that someone found the town doctor locked up in his own surgery. That discovery spurred some public-spirited citizens to break open the bank. And a red-faced bank manager broke the news as his bonds were unravelled. By then Jake and Fran were well clear of the abandoned surrey, and far from the regular trail. A long way away.

3

'Oh shucks,' the old man said, rolling off the woman's amply-round body. 'I don't know what's wrong with me. Mebbe I'm getting too old. I've heard tell that happens.'

'Don't worry,' the woman whispered. 'You got lots left in you yet, you lecherous ram. More likely you've drunk too much. It happens that way too.'

Eyes closed, he giggled drunkenly. 'Yeah. Must admit I've put some liquor down my scrawny neck tonight.'

'At least you did manage to perform once earlier in the evening.' She was exaggerating. The flicker inside her had been hardly perceptible but she was in the business of making men feel good.

'Yeah, I did, didn't I?' he mouthed proudly. 'You're right, there's still a bit of life in the old goat yet.'

She pulled her gown around her naked body and they lay silently in the semi-darkness. Then she said, 'Well, It's getting late. I'm going to have a last drink before I turn in. You want one?'

'If I have another I won't be able to find my way back to my rounder's cot.'

'Believe me, with or without another drink you'd have trouble making it to your bunk. It's OK. You can sleep here.'

'Miss Fifi, you're a doll and no mistake.'

She stood up and crossed to the table. As she poured a couple of shots of whiskey she caught sight of herself in the mirror. Doll, he'd called her. She wished it was true but it was only the booze talking. She'd never seen a doll with the puffed eyes and sagging cheeks that she could see before her. She told herself that it was the low-kerosene lamplight being unflattering; but she knew better. Her client had expressed concern with his age. Difficult to pinpoint with any accuracy but she put him, maybe, around seventy. For herself, only in her mid-thirties, she was concerned with her age too. Less because of her job, more that women seemed to concern themselves with the physical effects of age sooner than men.

No, she didn't need looks for her job. As mistress of the house she rarely attended to clients directly nowadays; but she had catered to the old man the last time he had passed through Arrowhead. It had been a couple of years ago but he had remembered her and asked for her specifically. The dear old soul had remembered her name too. She passed him his glass. He could only manage a sip and clumsily handed it back.

'Come here, baby. Just let me hold you.'

She put his glass back on the table. 'All right.

But I'm just going downstairs to make sure everything's locked up and all the johns are on their
way.'

She tied the gown around her and made the
rounds, saying goodnight to her girls. She'd
thought she was entering the real world when she
left the farm to become an abigail – but she
learned a hell of a sight more, once she'd given up
skivvying.

As she returned to the bedroom she could hear
rain beginning to flick the windowpane. She
finished her own drink and glanced briefly
between the curtains at the dark, wet street, then
turned out the argand lamp. She lay down on the
bed, snuggling her back into the man who
enveloped her in his arms, sighing contentedly as
he did so.

Constance Shaw, now known to the world as
Fifi, was the eldest of four girls. Her parents had
been settlers with a little homestead, out near
Monument, and for many years she had been the
only child. A young child was not to know the hard
work that went into such things and all she could
remember of those early years was glorious
summers and happiness. Sometimes after supper
her pa would light up his pipe and doodle tunes
on his accordion. Then, the mother had sliced
herself with a knife during kitchen chores. Didn't
seem too bad at the time but the wound turned
gangrenous and she had died, younger at her final
day than her daughter Constance was now.

After a while her father had married again and

the new family unit increased with three more
girls. With a gap of over fifteen years between
them, Constance had seen herself more as mother
than a sister. But happy times had returned
again. She remembered evenings when their
father supplied musical accompaniment while the
girls danced in the firelight. She smiled when she
recalled how he would admonish them when they
asked him to get out the old squeezebox. 'It's an
accordion, not an old squeezebox!'

Meg was the only one who persevered at learning how to play the thing, whatever it was called,
and eventually she was adept enough to knock
out a recognisable tune. So proficient did she
become that during birthday celebrations and
other festive occasions she would play while ma
and pa danced. More happy times. But there was
a succession of bad seasons and it was a strain for
one man to put food in six mouths, so the matur-
ing Constance had left to take up domestic service
with a well-to-do family in the nearby town. But
fate had another nasty trick up its sleeve and a
cholera outbreak took her father. The mother
couldn't cope and Constance felt obliged to send
money, but her servanting covered little more
than her own board.

Then something happened so that she was
unable even to send her paltry dollars. One day
the son of the family for whom she worked, thinking they were alone, had caught her in a bedroom
and, despite her protestations had forced her onto
the bed, tearing at her clothes. However, his

mother *had* been in the house and, hearing the commotion, had burst in upon the scene to see the girl's young body exposed. She blamed Constance for playing the temptress and dismissed her on the spot.

The girl was on the street, nowhere to live and only a handful of dollars and cents in her purse. Worse, her former mistress had quickly spread the word of her 'character', removing her prospects of further work in that line locally. She dearly wished to return home but, not wishing to put a further load on her step-mother, she just moved on and on till her money ran out. It was in a town called Arrowhead that she used up her last cents purchasing a meal. The town was small enough for knowledge of a newcomer to spread quickly. Especially when the stranger was a pretty young girl counting her pennies. Knowledge quickly reached the ears of a resident by the name of Smokey Sue who offered to take Constance under her wing. At first Constance was nonplussed by the comings and goings in the establishment that was her refuge, but she was learning fast about the world and this was another of her lessons. Smokey Sue, her appellation uniformly abridged to Smokey, was a madam and her place was the local whorehouse. Much to the chagrin of the Women's League, the place was called 'Christmas'. Smokey's attempt at wit – for the guys who passed through its entrance it was always Christmas.

It wasn't long before Smokey suggested a way

that the destitute Constance could solve her immediate financial problems. Constance's experiences were quickly hardening her and, although still an *ingénue* in a tough world, she had learned one thing. She did have something that could earn money. So, despite misgivings at first, she joined Smokey's small circle of sporting ladies. Following the practice of her new calling, she took a soubriquet. It was one of Smokey's little games to name her girls in alphabetical sequence. There being five doxies already under her wing her newest recruit entered the world's oldest profession as Fifi.

The cathouse boss had the authoritative demeanour that Constance had only witnessed before in men and, although croaky from the interminable cigarette hanging from her lip, her voice was sufficiently stentorian to keep any wayward johns in check. If she had a failing it was her penchant for some strange substance, virtually her only means of sustenance, which she ingested privately in her room and which would reduce her to extended periods of stupor. For a long time that didn't matter. What did matter was that she was kind to the girls, including the distraught penniless newcomer.

Thus, without telling her mother of the source, Constance could now send substantial regular payments back home. That was the pattern for a time, until she received word that the mother had died. Still young, the three girls were placed in an orphanage where Constance now sent money for the benefit of her sisters. Her innocence a distant memory, her new occupation taught her many things. The varied ways to physically please a man. And concomitant skills like how to handle drink. Her constitution seemed naturally impervious to the stuff and, following a drinking contest with her, there were many men whose last bleary-eyed sight from beneath the table had been Constance still standing with a drink in her hand.

And she'd also learned how to play cards. It had been that skill that had stood her in good stead when the old madam junkeyed away all the profits and could no longer pay the bills, even that of the girls. Knowing Constance was careful with her money, she had challenged the young woman to a game of cards during a slack period. Despite Constance's trying to talk her out of it the upshot of the long game was that the one-time serving wench won the cathouse called Christmas. Which was just as well because the old madam was becoming increasingly incapable through her habit, her intervals of narcotic-induced torpor increasing. Out of a mixture of gratitude and pity the young woman had kept her on without any duties until her chemical abuse eventually claimed her.

Constance gave her old saviour a decent burial and destroyed the accoutrements of addiction. During all this, she had had to learn new skills – managing, accounting, dealing with the obstreperous bank manager – and so efficient was she at the exercise that she had returned the business to a profitable concern. The place had run to seed during Smokey's last drug-fuelled years but Constance put every spare dollar into repairs and sprucing up the décor.

With the old man quiet beside her, she lay in the darkness listening to the rain. Folks had been waiting for a change in the weather; it was good for the crops. But of more importance to her was how much the muddy boots would mess up her carpets the next day. But that was insignificant alongside the worry she had about her younger sisters.

Fran was now twenty and the other two were in their late teens. For some time Constance had been conscious of their being a liability to the orphanage. The money from community funds was hardly enough to fill small bellies and she doubted whether the amounts she sent were enough to make up the difference, even though she had increased the payments when she had taken over Christmas. She knew the orphanage would be looking for ways of divesting themselves of the growing encumbrances but it was difficult to place girls. One thing she knew, she didn't want them off-handedly thrown out and certainly not following the noisy debauch of her own occupation.

'Let you and I get married,' the oldster suddenly murmured behind her in the darkness, bringing her thoughts back to the present.

'I thought you were asleep,' she whispered.

'No, I mean it.'

'We girls get offers of marriage ten times a week,' she countered. 'Now go to sleep.'

'Naw, Fifi. I'm serious. Just because you can see my elbows through my sleeves you think I ain't worth much. I tell you, lady, I'm one of the richest guys around. I could look after you well.'

'Yeah, yeah,' she sighed. She'd heard it all before.

'Me and my pardner, we been working this gold-seam for years up in the Badrocks.' Drink and tiredness blurred his speech. 'Don't trust banks so we've hid the money in a cave near our workings. Couple of seasons back my sidekick, poor critter, died in a roof fall – so there's only me now. My memory plays tricks these days so I drew a map of where it is, 'case I forgot. All drawed out clear. The thing's in my warbag.' His voice got fainter as sleep grabbed at him. 'Believe me, gal, there's enough to see you and me into our old age.'

In her time she'd been promised everything from a ranch in Texas to the moon itself. This was a new one to add to the list, being promised a share in El Dorado.

'What do you say?' he said in slow, fading tones.

'Let's talk about it in the morning when you've sobered up,' she said, hoping that by then he would have forgotten it. Grateful that she could now hear only the spluttered breathing of drunken sleep she allowed her own brain to float out on the ocean of slumber.

She was awakened by gruntings and jerkings

beside her. 'What's the matter?' she asked. 'A bad dream?'

'No, no.' The words staccatoed out. 'Oh Christ.'

Not yet dawn; the old fellow was just a vague shape in the darkness. She rolled out of bed and fumbled for the matches, eventually lighting the kerosene. The old fellow was grimacing, eyes creased shut.

'What can I do?' she asked.

'Nothing, I think this is it.' He was having trouble getting the words out.

'I'll get you a glass of water.'

'No, no time. I've had it before. But never as bad as this. This is the big one.'

She rubbed at his chest around where his scrawny fingers were groping.

'Listen,' he whispered. 'Got no family, nobody. You been good to me, Fifi. Everything's yours. And don't forget the chart. It's yours.'

He went rigid, his back arching, his heels thrusting into the bed. His arms fell away and his body went limp, the only sound a long-drawn-out exhalation of breath that seemed to go on interminably until it faded.

She checked for pulse at wrist and throat, found none. She slapped at his face, rubbed his chest, his fingers. Nothing. She sat holding his hand as the first glimmer of day appeared at the gap between the curtains.

He was buried later that day in the cemetery up on the hill that overlooked Arrowhead. It was a simple affair with Constance the only mourner. She was not particularly religious and she didn't really know the old-timer but she felt there should be someone saying goodbye. It was short and quick with no hitch, save someone had told the Women's League Against Loose Morals about the circumstances of the death with the result that a couple of their members were on Main Street with their usual banners. They had been running a campaign to close the cathouse as long as she could remember.

Although the arrangements had been as simple as possible, there was not enough cash in the old man's wallet to cover the funeral so she gave his mule and tack to the undertaker.

'The tack ain't worth a cent,' the latter complained, 'and what am I gonna get for a flea-bitten pack-ass?' So she threw in a few dollars of her own to make up the difference in an attempt to shut up the moaning mortician. All she had left was the threadbare warbag and its redundant gewgaws. Why she didn't throw away the chart with the rest she didn't know. She didn't even open it, just abstractedly stashed it at the back of a drawer.

4

Before he knew what was happening Clay Morgan was flat on his back. As he stared at the cloudless sky, with the wind thumped out of him, he could hear Belle whinnying. Still dazed, he hauled himself to his feet and staggered to the stricken animal. He tried to pacify her by stroking her neck as he made an inspection. He'd heard the crack and had guessed the cause. She'd stepped in a gopher hole and broke her leg. Her cries were ear-splitting in the dry, hot air. Unsuccessfully he tried to stop her attempts to rise on the shattered limb. He looked across the salt licks. The town was still over five miles away. It would be nightfall before he could get back with help. Then, what help can you provide a horse with a broken leg? He knew one thing. After all the faithful service she had given him, he couldn't leave her like this, whinnying, baking in the heat for god knows how many hours. He owed her that much.

Sick at heart, he pulled his gun and stared at the cold, heartless metal of the barrel. Could he? They'd been together many years. Could he? He had to.

41

' 'Bye, old gal.' With that he raised the weapon.
She was oblivious of his action. Her beautiful
head rose and fell in her attempts to rise, her eyes
rolling. With difficulty he held her head down,
long enough to level the gun and pull the trigger.
The bullet smashed into the back of her skull
between the ears. She quivered and then was still.
He dropped to his knees and cradled her head.
'It's all over now, gal.' After a while, he extricated
the saddle and slung it over his shoulder. There
were tears in his eyes as he began the homeward
trek.

Junction City was what happens at the end of
the railroad when the trains don't come any
more. Its name, faded on the angled, rotting sign
that he passed as he trudged into town, was false
advertising on two counts. Junction – there were
no trails in or out; and there was no railroad, the
tracks bypassing the place by at least twenty
miles. City was a misnomer too – even by frontier ass-end-of-nowhere standards it was barely
a town. Didn't even have a telegraph. But
Junction City was what folk still called it, the
few folk who were left, that was. He heavy-footed
along the drag that separated the two rows of
false fronts and headed for a shack labelled LAW
OFFICE, SHERIFF CLAY MORGAN. He dropped the
saddle behind his desk and went to the livery
stable.

'Hi, Ike,' he said to the old ostler who was
polishing a harness.

'Hi, Sheriff. What can I do for you this fine morning?'

'It's not quite so fine, Ike. Had a mishap. Belle broke a leg out on the flats. Had to put her away.'

The man stopped work, 'Jeez, I'm sorry, Clay. She was a beautiful animal.'

'Yah, near broke my heart to do it.'

'Had her a long time too.'

'Yeah. Bought her when I ran the store. Remember?'

The old man nodded. 'Of course I remember. You bought her from me. Now you sit yourself down, pardner. I've got some coffee brewing.'

A minute later they'd each got a steaming cup of Java in front of them. 'And what were you doing out on the flats?' Ike asked.

'Couple of homesteaders out there were butting heads over water rights. One of the hands rode in at sun-up to tell me about the fracas. By the time I'd made it out there the heat had gone out of the argument. So, I got 'em to shake on an agreement and now they're old buddies again.'

'And you had the accident on the way back?'

Clay nodded. Then, 'Listen, Ike, I'd like to ask you a favour. I need to go back to the flats to bury her. Can I borrow Star?'

'Of course you can. Come out and see him.'

Clay followed the old-timer out to the lodge-pole corral. The young black stallion ambled over to the fence and took the carrot that his owner offered.

'You know, from a distance they could be the same animal,' Clay said.

'Well, as mother and son there ought to be some similarities.'

The lawman stroked the animal's muzzle. 'A horse is just supposed to be a tool. But Belle was more than that to me. Something special.'

Ike patted the neck of the young stallion. 'And so's he.'

'I'm gonna be needing a new mount. Would you consider selling him?'

The ostler pondered. 'Suppose I would be aiming to sell him eventually. I'm gonna have to pull up my picket pin sometime. Don't need to have much of a brain to know the town's on its last legs.'

'How much would you be asking?'

'I gotta be frank, Clay. He's a good horse and represents my grubstake to get out of here. So I would need a hundred.'

Clay whistled. 'A hundred?'

'I don't have to tell you he's a horse in a thousand. He's got speed and staying power – just like his dam. He's good breeding-stock too.'

Clay couldn't argue with the reasoning but the figure was a shock. He patted the horse once more. 'I've got to see the missus and attend to things. I'll be back directly.'

'Meantimes, I'll get Star ready.'

Liz was working in the kitchen. She turned her head away in rejection of his greeting kiss and carried on with her chores. 'You think more of that damn horse than you do of me,' she said after he'd relayed his news.

'Is that all you got to say?' he asked.

She ignored his question, 'Well, what you gonna do now? What good's a sheriff without a horse?' She pondered on her own question. 'Huh,' she continued, 'about as good as a storekeeper without a store, that's what.' She knew that barb would get to him and she looked at him for a reaction but he gave none. 'Well, what you gonna do?' she went on. 'We haven't got any spare cash for no darned new horse, that's for sure.'

'First off, I'm gonna see Wilder,' he said. 'He's not only mayor and chairman of the council but he holds the money strings in the town. I'll see what he can come up with. He set up the job of sheriff. He's my boss. It's up to him to solve the problem.'

She made a dismissive noise. 'Huh. Mr Wilder's not interested. You're window-dressing. That piece of tin on your chest is just for show. He doesn't want you to actually do anything as the sheriff.'

'Yeah, I know the job is largely a front of respectability for his town council. Having our own law deters the county authorities from taking over. But it is a job and as long as I hold the post I'm gonna do it properly. And I have to have a means for getting about. That needs money.'

He made for the door and opened it.

'Where are you going?' she asked.

'To see him. He does run the bank after all, so there's dough there.'

'Mr Wilder won't thank you for bothering him.'

'Mebbe I can come to some arrangement with him.'

'What kind of arrangement?'

'A loan, something like that,' he said as he crossed the doorway.

'Oh no,' he heard her shout after him. 'No loans, Clay Morgan. That's tantamount to spending our money before we get it.'

The owner of Junction City's one and only bank was standing at the counter drumming his fingers. His stomach rumbled, prompting him to look at the clock. Nearly lunch time.

Some years ago J. P. Wilder, wheeler-dealer *extraordinaire*, had acquired inside knowledge on the planned route of the Sante Fe Railroad. A one-time accomplice ensconced in head office had allowed him access to the plan of the projected route. It had meant slipping a small fortune into the guy's back pocket, as the details on that paper were as guarded as the crown jewels of England. On the strength of it Wilder had moved out in advance and established Junction City. Up till then there'd only been a scatter of dirt-farmers scratching a living from the bleak terrain, but some folks believed in his dream and followed him out. He thought up the grandiose name for the site and the once deserted stretch of sand became a hive of activity with building upwards and outwards. Word of the boom spread and others came in their droves.

Only snag was, it looked like the two-timer had

been finally two-timed himself. Somebody had been pushing even more dollars into back pockets because, when the railroad eventually did come, it skirted some twenty miles to the north, leaving Junction City once more a nowhere place. And the boom, which had thrived solely on expectation, now only had itself to feed on. Then, just as quickly as the balloon had been pumped up, it burst. Junction City's version of the old saying – from shirtsleeves to shirtsleeves in three generations – was more merciless. From shirtsleeves to holes in the elbows in a mere two seasons. Folks drifted, moved on, to leave a shell whose only *raison d'etre* was supplying dirt farmers.

Wilder had been in a quandary. He couldn't just move out with his belongings in a wagon like the others. Maybe the place was a hollowed shell – but it was his. The way he saw it he had invested too much to quit. Aiming to make the best of a bad job he changed tack and set about using strong-arm methods to make it a one-company town. A town in which he owned all the businesses, lock, stock and peppercorn barrel. The way he saw it, what little cash there was to make would be his.

At the time Clay Morgan had run a dry-goods store and was the only tradesman who held out against the big man. He'd learned about book-keeping and handling supplies during his army stint in the quartermaster's store. He enjoyed the work and, although it didn't make much, he owned the store outright and it provided a living. So he refused to sell or be scared off. The situation stayed that way till one day his store got burned down, leaving him destitute. Like everybody else in town, he knew it was Wilder's doing but he couldn't prove it. Wilder even used the circumstance to raise his own public image. If there'd been a sheriff, Wilder had said sanctimoniously, it wouldn't have happened. Under the auspices of the town council and, feigning pity for the hapless couple, he offered Clay the post. The man wasn't awed by the prospect. He could ride and had learned how to handle a gun as a soldier. The pay was peanuts but Clay had a wife to look after. So with nothing else going for him, he accepted.

As the banker caressed his rumbling stomach, the door clattered open.

'Ah, Clay,' he said when he saw the sheriff coming through the door. 'Come into the office,' he went on, 'I been fixing on seeing you.' He crossed to the door, locked it and turned the sign to CLOSED. 'I was closing for lunch anyhows.'

When they were seated opposite each other in the back office he appraised his visitor. 'You're looking a mite trail-dusty.'

'Yeah. Fact is, Mr Wilder, I've had a mishap. Lost my horse. Out on the flats. She took a tumble down a gopher hole. Leg broke. Had to put her out of her misery.' He sighed at the thought. 'So, I'm looking for a replacement. That's why I'm here. I was wondering if the town council would stand the bill for a new mount. You being the head of the council and a banker and all.'

The moneyman studied his visitor further.

'Clay, I'm sorry to say, it just ain't your day. We, the town council that is, had an emergency meeting this morning. With times being bad and folks still leaving, our tax revenue is down. That's why I wanted to see you. You know taxes are where your wages come from. With the take declining, there's nothing for it but for you to take a wage cut.'

Clay threw back his head. 'Jeez, it never rains but it pours.'

'We can manage to pay you at your present rate for the next month,' the banker added, then pulled a wry face. 'But after that . . .'

'Cut by how much?'

'We figure ten per cent. But I'm afraid it could be more.'

'Hell's teeth, Mr Wilder. Liz and I can hardly manage as it is.'

'I can imagine. But, Clay, times are bad for all of us.'

The lawman glanced around the plush office, then appraised the large cigar the banker was just lighting, and he tried to figure out who 'us' was.

'So you see,' the man said after he'd successfully fired his tobacco, 'there's no way we can foot an unexpected bill for a new set of horse legs.'

The other ruminated on it. 'OK, what about a loan? I do need a horse.'

'Even if you got the money, where you gonna get another horse? Ain't an available horse left in town that I know of. It'd mean travelling half-way across the territory to buy one – and paying a fancy city price too.'

'No. There is *one* in town. Old Isaac's got a young stallion over at the livery. In fact the son of the mare I've lost. He's asking a hundred dollars.'

'A hundred bucks!'

'It's a good horse, Mr Wilder. And the only one in town.'

'This is a bank, Clay. Run on banking principles. What could you put up as collateral? You ain't got no property now your store's gone.'

The lawman thought about it. 'The horse itself. That would be what you call collateral.'

'Clay, I can see you don't know much about the practice of banking. That wouldn't constitute collateral. What would happen to the bank's investment if you put it down another gopher hole? What's happened once can happen again. I run a business. I've got to have security. And a horse ain't security. Plus, I've got to show some kind of profit on the arrangement. On top of that, with your forthcoming cut in wages I figure you'd have the devil's own job trying to meet the interest charges, never mind the repayments.'

Clay said nothing and the banker, with a tone of finality in his voice, added, 'It's a harsh world but that's the way it works.'

The lawman stood up and paced the room. 'Well, I'll tell you something else about the way the world works: in a territory like this a sheriff ain't no good without a horse.'

'I'm sorry, Clay, you'll just have to do the best

you can with what you've got.' He rose. 'Now, if you'll excuse me I've got an appointment with my lunch over at the eats house.'

Clay accompanied the man outside onto the boardwalk. He waved his arm along the main drag. 'And what if some opportunist desperado comes riding in, pulls a gun and makes you clean out your safe. As the sheriff, how the hell am I expected to light out after him without a horse?'

The banker locked the door, 'An opportunist bankrobber? Unlikely. Even I have to admit it – this place is nowheres-ville. Nobody's gonna ride out here looking for easy money. You know it's never happened before. What's more, nobody can get in that safe other than me. Have you seen the size of it? On top of that, I've got a gun in my drawer, and one in the safe. I think I could cope with such an unlikely eventuality,'

'Bank robbing ain't unknown even in off-the-beaten-track places like this, Mr Wilder. And what happens if you didn't cope and I need to get on the varmint's trail?'

'Clay,' the man said, shaking his head condescendingly, 'we'll cross that bridge if ever we should come to it. Now, if you'll excuse me, my ulcer's rumbling.'

Clay returned home and relayed the conversation to his wife. Liz sat down and clenched her hands. 'I married you when I thought you were going somewhere. But you can't do a darned thing right. No matter which way you cut it, you always come up with empty hands. You lose the business, the only chance we had. Now look at you. Just about enough money to put beans on the table. A sheriff with no horse, and now you tell me your pay's going to be cut.'

'I still need a horse, Liz.'

'Well, you can't get a loan, and we wouldn't be able to handle the debt anyway. You gotta face it, Clay; we haven't even saved enough to have a bank account. All we got is a few dollars in a pot at the back of the cupboard.'

'Yeah, I know, sweet.' He sighed deeply, then added, 'Anyways, listen. I'm gonna be gone for a few hours. I got some burying to do.'

Over at the livery stable, Star was saddled up and Ike was dressed for riding. 'I'm coming with you,' the old man said. 'You're gonna need another pair of hands. No mean task, burying a horse.'

'Two of us? How we gonna get out there? There's only one horse in town.'

The elder man grinned. 'Star is a strong animal. He can carry two, no sweat.'

Hours later the job was done. As Ike had said, it was no mean task burying several hundred-weight of horse – even with a pair of shovels wielded by two sets of hands.

5

The waterspout was already being swung into position over the engine when the couple dismounted from the railroad car. An attendant passed down their baggage. Jake rewarded him with some coins and picked up the two heavier cases, while Fran handled a smaller valise. At the edge of the town proper they paused, laying down their traps, and looked the place over: an unremarkable avenue of false fronts.

'That looks like a hotel,' Jake said, indicating a more substantial two-storey building half-way down the drag.

Along the boardwalk they passed a line of seated idlers. Most were oldsters past their working lives. One was shy of a leg; another was slumped in a wheelchair with a blanket around him. Some touched their hats to the passing lady while others just continued with their talking, smoking and watching the world go by. As they made their way Jake noted the disposition of places: saloons, drugstore and other emporia.

They registered at the hotel as Mr and Mrs Lee

Holland and took occupancy of their room. After a wash-up and a meal, they returned to their room and Jake spread his map over the bed to study. Towns were circled tracing out a staggered trajectory over the document. He'd invested a whole season crossing the territory, picking out the best targets and casing the joints. Their backtrail was marked by crosses pinpointing accomplished business.

'Well, so far so good, baby,' he said. 'That's where we are now.' His finger marked a point, then swept along the chart. 'And our next job is the bank in Hondo Bend, there, the other side of Prairie City. But its handling's gonna need some cogitating on. We can't pull the smallpox trick again. News will probably have spread about that stunt.'

He was thinking aloud and didn't expect any contribution from his companion. 'There's two problems,' he went on. 'It's an isolated place so we can't just hit the bank and get out quick. They've got a good lawman. I figured that the last time I was here. Reckon he could be mighty quick in rounding up a posse.' He scanned the map. 'And out there, there's desert in all directions. It'd need expert horsemen to keep ahead of a posse – whichever way we lit out. The other snag is, the place is too small for a couple of strangers to hide up in.'

'Sounds too difficult if you ask me.'

'Well, I ain't asking you.'

'Still, sounds difficult.' She peered over his

shoulder. 'For Chrissakes, we've hit every big place in the territory. Haven't we got enough now? The saddlebags are full of money.'

'Jake Bridger's never got enough,' he said, without turning his head.

She considered the scrawls on the map. 'Seems to me, maybe we should pick something easier.'

'Nothing's too difficult, woman. Just needs brains. The Hondo Bend bank is too rich a plum to ignore. Miles from anywhere, it's the only bank in the area. That means rich pickings. And never been hit. Nobody is expecting it. All we need is a good cover.'

He looked at his companion while he thought. 'Cover,' he mused. 'Now, if you ain't seen in the bank during the job, you wouldn't be suspected, so you'd be OK. That leaves me. It'd have to be me who's disguised. That way we could remain unsuspected in the hotel until the heat was off. But disguised as what?'

He lit a cigarette while he pondered further. 'Yeah. We ride into town with me in some masquerade get-up and we book in at the hotel. We bide our time for a spell then, undisguised but wearing a bandanna over my kisser, I knock off the bank. Then I cut back to you in the hotel and re-adopt my camouflage. Mmm, but my disguise has to be so good that nobody would suspect. Needs thinking out. But we got time to think up something good. No sense in rushing.'

What happened the next day might have been

deemed by some to be an accident. In one sense it was but in another it wasn't, as Jake's mind was forever tuned to take advantage of chance events. He was coming out of the saloon having picked up twenty dollars playing cards. The local bonos were easy meat to card-sharping and he could have taken much more but he was just killing time and didn't want to arouse suspicions.

On his way back to the hotel he noted a crowd on the boardwalk on the other side of the drag a few blocks down from the saloon.

'What's happened?' he asked a bystander.

'Looks like Old Man Rudge's finally cashed in his chips. A mercy really. The poor feller's had a miserable life these past few years. It'll be a release for his missus. She's been the one who's had to take the brunt.'

'How come?'

'Some seasons ago he fell from a horse. Paralysed down one side of his body. Reduced to a vegetable in a wheelchair.'

'Yeah,' Jake said. 'Saw the guy when we came into town.'

'His missus had to dress him, feed him, wash him,' the other continued. 'She's been a tower of strength but it must have took its toll on the old gal; she's not getting any younger. Used to wheel out what was left of poor Ben every day to sit with the oldsters in the sun. Well, he's finally pegged it.'

Jake leant on the rail, lit a cigarette and watched. The slumped figure, legs covered by a blanket, was wheeled away while a bevy of elderly ladies comforted his distraught widow. By the time the crowd had dispersed, Jake had had the idea he had been waiting for.

The funeral was the next day. From a seat on the boardwalk Jake watched the sorry-looking procession wend its way out to the cemetery. In the interests of decorum he left it for a day before he knocked on the widow's door.

He took off his hat when she appeared.

'The name's Holland, ma'am, ' he said. 'Lee Holland. I'd like to offer my condolences on the passing of Mr Rudge. I didn't know him but the fellers say he was a good man.'

'That's very kind of you, Mr Holland. Yes, he was a good man.'

He nodded and paused a few seconds before continuing. 'I know it's a bad time for you, ma'am and, if I'm speaking out of turn, why, you just tell me and I'll make myself scarce. You don't know me, ma'am. I just happen to be passing through town and I witnessed the tragic event. See, I'm returning home to Garret. You might know the place. Some fifty miles due south of here.'

'Oh yes, I have heard of Garrett, of course. But I have never been out that way. Ben and I never had time to travel much.'

'Well we run a small beef ranch out there. The fact is, Pa had an accident – got trampled by a wayward cow – and has been bedridden for years. I remembered your dear husband's wheelchair and it occurred to me that would be a way of getting Pa out into the sunshine. We live way out in the wilds and there ain't no way of getting such a chair. As I said, you tell me if I'm speaking out of turn at such a time – but would you be willing to sell the chair? I know it'll have sentimental associations for you and so I'll understand if you tell me to be on my way.'

Her face brightened. 'That's a splendid idea. The thing looks so forlorn sitting there without him and I know Ben would be happy to know it's providing use and pleasure to someone else.'

'Name a figure, ma'am.'

'No, I wouldn't dream of it. You can have it for free. It would do my heart good too, knowing it was still serving some useful purpose.'

Jake didn't show his satisfaction at the outcome, simply saying, 'Well, maybe I could make a donation to your favourite charity.'

'That's another wonderful idea, Mr Holland. We have a fund for putting up some kind of recreational building alongside the chapel. We are staunch Methodists and, as you probably know, our church is strongly against gambling. The playing of cards seems to entice so many of the town's menfolk that we hope to provide them with alternative, more godly, leisure pursuits. Maybe you could put a few coins in the fund for the building.'

'I'd be more than happy to, ma'am.' He thrust

his hand into his pocket and pulled out his black-
jack winnings. 'Twenty dollars sound OK?'

By the time he had got back to the hotel he had
worked out a plan. 'I'll buy a wagon,' he explained
to his companion. 'I need somewhere to dress up,
a place where nobody's watching, so suspicions
aren't aroused. A small covered wagon will fit the
bill. I've seen one alongside the livery at the end
of town. We'll leave town in the wagon and I
change on the way. Two towns on, there's a stage
halt, Prairie City. We dump the wagon and take
the stage from there to Hondo Bend.' He uncurled
some money from his billfold. 'Buy a blanket,
something to cover my legs, make me look like an
invalid. And get yourself some fancy clothes. A
bonnet too.'

'Do I need a disguise?'

'Not a complete one. But it won't come amiss if
you change your appearance a mite.'

6

Constance had been right about the rain resulting in mud on the thick-pile carpets of the whore-house known as Christmas. It was several days on from the death of the old-timer and the downpour had finally ceased but the main drag was still a quagmire. She'd arranged for sheets of paper to be laid on the floor during working hours and for clients to leave their boots in the lobby but it wasn't long before the paper got churned up and drunken brushpoppers ignored the requests to divest themselves of their footwear.

It was mid-morning and, having arranged for Little Jim the coloured houseboy to set about the task, she was in her office looking at the Christmas accounts when there came a shout from the lobby.

'Miss Fifi, visitors are messing up the floor again.'

She cursed, closed her account book and went into the lobby. It was the mayor, sheriff and a couple of black-clothed women. Constance looked at their boots and the trail of fresh mud they had brought in.

61

'Oh Charlie, can't you see we're trying to keep the place clean?'

'Never mind that,' the mayor said. He was trying to put firmness into his voice but there was an air of uncertainty about him. 'We've come on important business.'

'What kind of business?'

'It's the sheriff here,' one of the bluestockings squawked, nodding at the lawman. 'He's serving you a notice to quit.'

'I don't understand,' Constance queried.

The mayor threw a glance at the houseboy. 'Do we talk here or have you got somewhere more private?'

She gave the dignitary and sheriff a patronizing look, each in turn. 'Come, come. Charlie, Fred, as regular visitors, you both know we got places more private.'

The mayor noisily cleared his throat; the lawman shuffled his feet, while their lady companions looked sniffily away – only to find their gaze falling upon the erotica decorating the walls.

'This way,' Constance said, conducting them into her office. 'Now what is this all about, Charlie?'

The mayor looked embarrassed. 'Fact of the matter is, Fifi, from midnight next Saturday the town of Arrowhead comes under the jurisdiction of the county. That means all county laws and by-laws will be operative here.' He indicated for the sheriff to continue.

'Arrowhead has been a boom town,' the lawman went on. 'It's grown faster than law and order.'

'Yes,' one of the women smirked. 'Now law and order is catching up.'

The lawman shut her up with a dismissive hand. 'The matter which affects you is that there's a county ordinance forbidding houses of ill repute. You gotta close down, Fifi.'

The proprietress dropped into her chair while she absorbed the statement.

'Is this on the square? It's not another trick by the Women's League? They've been trying to close this place since the days of Adam.'

'It's on the square, Fifi,' the lawman said, almost apologetically.

She thought on it. 'Is there some right of appeal?'

'Afraid not. It's a rock-solid county law.'

'What about the girls? What they gonna do?'

'They're gonna have to leave town,' the mayor said. 'I got the news first thing this morning and I called an extraordinary town meeting. The Women's League were insistent you and the girls left as part of the deal.'

Constance nodded. 'So, the good ladies of the community have finally won. What's this about a deal?'

'The lawyer on the council pointed out there could be legal ramifications of your eviction, there being a deed and all. So the meeting came up with the idea of compulsory purchase. If you agree to leave on the noon stage tomorrow the council will buy the place.

That way it's all legal, fair and square.'

'They mention a price?'

'Two grand.'

'Two grand? Everything I've got's tied up in this place. You know it's worth more than that, Charlie.'

'Two grand. That's the figure. Be fair, Fifi. The way I heard it you only picked the place up in a card game.'

'How I came to be the legal owner is neither here nor there.' She pondered for a moment, then asked, 'And what do the girls get in this scheme of things?'

'Nothing. They don't come into it. You're the one with the deeds.'

'And you're happy to see a bunch of girls pushed out of town with just a few cents in their pockets?'

'The girls are your responsibility, Fifi. How you split the money is up to you. But if you play awkward you'll be forcibly evicted and be leaving with nothing.'

'Two grand?' Constance repeated disdainfully. Then she nodded. 'I see it all now. Frank Benson, the hotel man, is on the council. Figure this is his way of picking up another hotel cheap.'

'It's nothing to do with Benson.'

'The hell it ain't.' She shook her head. 'And what about the furniture? All imported. That alone's worth two grand.'

'The furniture wasn't mentioned in our discussions. Reckon you'll be allowed to take what you can.'

'How the hell am I gonna shift out a whole set of furniture?'

'Ain't my problem, Fifi. Remember, noon tomorrow.'

With that, the delegation left. Constance trailed behind them into the lobby and watched them exit. 'You can forget the cleaning up, Little Jim. Tell the girls I want to see them.'

Minutes later she related the news to the assembled group, told them of the deadline. Some cried, the others comforted them.

'What about money?' one asked. 'How am I going to get by? I don't know about the other girls but I haven't saved much, Miss Fifi.'

'Don't worry,' she concluded. 'I'll see to it that you don't leave empty-handed. I'll give you what's owed and some more. Now I suggest you close up your affairs and make necessary preparations.'

When they had gone she sat at her desk and thought over the matter. With everybody with clout against her, there was nothing she could do. She thought through the practicalities. There was a few hundred in the cashbox and a grand or more in the bank. She would hold an auction of the furniture and whatever else wasn't nailed down. That would provide more cash. But after that, what to do, where to go? She walked slowly up the stairs with the intention of sorting out her clothing. By the time she had crossed the landing she had decided her course of action.

She'd travel to the orphanage and get her sisters out of the place. After she'd divvied up with

the Christmas girls, she'd still have a good
amount in her purse. Enough maybe for her to
open some kind of store for all her sisters to work
in. A ladies' clothing emporium perhaps. Trouble
was the stagecoach, on which the Christmas girls
would be leaving, was westbound and the orphanage was to the east. That meant catching the train
and that wasn't due till the morning after. She'd
need a time extension on the deadline she'd been
given. She went to the law office and explained
the problem.

Thankfully the sheriff was alone and not now
under the eagle eyes of the Women's League. He
kicked it around his brain for a moment. As a
regular after-hours customer of the Christmas he
was stuck between two camps. 'OK, Fifi, for old
time's sake I'll take the responsibility to give you
permission to stay over one more day. The
mayor'll condone that. And I should be able to
square it with the do-gooders.'

One more day. That fitted her plans even better.
Gave her a little extra time having the place to
herself.

She stepped onto the boardwalk outside the law
office, hiding a smile. Right, she'd got two days to
sort things out.

On the final day she made her morning toilet with
the fastidiousness of a débutante attending her
first ball. The bluestockings of the Women's
League would like to see her skulking out of town
like a hounded rat but she did not intend giving

them the satisfaction. Confident in her plans, she hummed as she looked this way and that in the mirror, giving her face a final once-over. The previous day she had held an impromptu auction of the furniture and got $500. Along with the money from the bank, the cash assets had totalled over four grand, which she split fifty-fifty with the girls. After tearful goodbyes she had seen them off on the noon stage.

The two grand that she was left with should be enough to set up her sisters. Things were looking up. Even the rain hadn't returned and, after a couple of days of sunshine, there was no mud to spoil her exit.

She pursed her lips at the mirror once more, and then donned a saffron dress with matching coat and lappeted bonnet. Outside, the Women's League was waiting for her. She ignored them and opened a parasol which she began to spin gently over her shoulder as she walked across the sun-baked street to the station. Along the way she picked up a retinue of sightseers; at least the women amongst them eager to see the back of her. They whispered amongst themselves, each aware that her departure would be the topic of conversation for weeks to come. She paid them no heed, sweeping along like a queen, her pert nose lifted. Yes, they would remember her departure all right.

Little Jim was waiting for her at the station, having earlier brought her traps. In front of a gloating audience she gave him a hug and slipped some bills in his hand.

'Be a good boy for your ma,' she whispered, 'and remember what I said. Don't go back to the Christmas. It doesn't belong to us any more and it's all locked up. Remember, don't go back. Promise.'

'Yes, ma'am.'

It wasn't because it was locked up that she had been so insistent that he keep away, but that was all the explanation she was giving him. Shortly the bellstacker clanked to a standstill and Little Jim helped the conductor load her luggage. As the train pulled out she leaned her head against the backrest and closed her eyes. She hadn't slept much for two nights and her head was still in a whirl at the notion of how quickly the circumstances of one's life could change.

As the train picked up speed she revelled in the notion of seeing her sisters again. And never once did she look back at the receding town of Arrowhead. In her book it was already history.

The train had disappeared when the gossiping crowd returned to Main Street and someone shouted 'Fire'. Flames were licking through the windows of the building that bore the name of Christmas. There was little chance of saving the place. The candle she'd left burning amongst the oil-soaked rags and lumber in the cellar had finally done its trick.

The woman once known as Fifi had a soft side. But she had a hard side too.

7

A dust-covered Concord rolled into Hondo Bend. The whip hauled on the reins and slammed on the brake. He worked his aching shoulders, instructed his buddy to unfasten the wheelchair from the roof rack, then wearily eased himself to the ground. He opened the door and lowered the drop-step. A drummer and cattleman stepped down to the sandy earth and went their ways. The driver assisted the bonneted young lady to alight, then helped his companion to lower the wheelchair and carry it to the boardwalk.

Together they carried the elderly-looking gentleman out of the stage and carefully sat him in the chair. The young lady adjusted the blanket around the invalid's legs and thanked the men with some coins.

'Thank you, ma'am,' the driver said, touching his hat. 'Your connecting stage comes through in three days. Meanwhiles, I can recommend the Plains Hotel yonder.'

The couple signed in as father and daughter and were given connecting rooms. Because of the old man's invalidity, they requested they take their meals in their rooms.

First Jake and then the baggage were carried upstairs. He waited until his helpers had returned downstairs, then he locked the doors, walking gently to obviate any heavy footedness on the boards that might be perceived below.

'My door always stays locked,' he whispered, after he'd allocated rooms. 'Anyone comes nosing, and they will do when the heat's on, they'll have to come through you first. When they do, give me time to make myself presentable.'

Unwrapping the muffler that had obscured much of his face he crossed to the window.

'Just as I'd hoped,' he said, taking in the main street from behind a side curtain. 'I can see the bank from here. Everything's working out jim-dandy.'

He went to the back window. Outside, it was deserted. 'Good,' he said. 'That's the one thing I was worried about. But it's no problem. Gonna be easy to get out and back.'

He returned and looked around the room, nodding towards the bed. 'OK, anyone calls unexpectedly and I ain't disguised, I wrap myself up in the bed,' he said. 'And you tell 'em I ain't very well.'

With that he relieved himself of his disguise. First off was the hat with its white horsehair tresses glued round the inside band. Then, he carefully removed the false beard, likewise made of horsehair. Finally he washed the hardened glue from his face and shaved.

'It's a small town,' he said, his face reflecting the satisfaction he felt as he ran his fingers over his once-again smooth features. 'Word will have gotten around about a spavined old coot being in town. Get down to the town and find what stands for a drug-store in this God-forsaken place and buy a bottle of painkiller. Say your pa's old joints are giving him gyp. That'll help keep the charade going.'

She went to the door but instead of leaving, turned, deposited herself on a chair and looked at him.

'What's the matter with you?' he growled. 'I gave you a job to do.'

'What happened to Bess and Meg?'

'Jesus! I've told you to stop pestering me about them.'

'They're my sisters I want to know about them. I got a right to know.'

'History, that's what they are.'

'History? What does that mean? Are they all right? That's all I want to know.'

'They was, last time I saw 'em. That's all I know. Now shut up about 'em and get downstairs and start acting the part of a dutiful daughter after some painkiller for her ailing pa.'

Jake spent the next day at the window of the hotel watching the bank. He already knew its layout, having cased the joint many months previously. Under pretence of some trivial cash business, he had wised himself up on the interior: the counter across the front of the lobby, the gate at the end that allowed access to the back. He had spied the safe in the backroom. Then he'd examined the back of the building. Worked out how he could return to the hotel, north along the back edge of the building line, across the drag at the far end of town and along the backs again south. Just as important, as with all target towns, he'd located the law office.

Now, from his high vantage point, he was more concerned with the bank's routine. Nothing had changed. There was the manager, an aging paunchy individual, and an assistant, a scrawny young man with pebble glasses.

He expected no trouble from either. He could tell by the fall of their clothing that neither carried a hidden gun. He knew there would be at least one gun on the premises but as hired hands the two pen-pushers would not have what it takes to defend money that was not theirs. Through his travels and keeping up to date via the newspapers, he knew the disposition of banks in the territory and their histories. As far as he knew, this one had never been knocked over. That would make them complacent and without the experience or nerve to stand up to a hardcase with a gun.

As he had observed on his previous exploratory visit, they still opened at nine and closed at four like clockwork.

The only one in town that concerned him was the sheriff. With a rep as a no-nonsense lawman he was one of the reasons no heist merchants had tried the bank before. And that was the reason Jake made it his business to keep tabs on the guy's where-at, as much as he could from the refuge of the curtain.

He took out a little notebook in which he had recorded all information he deemed relevant and turned the pages till he found what he was looking for.

'It's got to be tomorrow,' he said. 'It's three days before the stage comes through. We'll have to lie doggo for a day. Can't be helped but it might arouse suspicions if we left on the same day as the job.'

He spent the next day again at the window, noting nothing untoward. Even better he'd seen the sheriff go to the law office for his afternoon coffee, as was his habit.

Nearing closing time, he took his shoulder holster from his baggage.

'You said there'd be no shooting,' Fran said as she watched him strap the contrivance around his chest.

'Don't worry. This is just so that the critters see my point of view.' He pulled on a large jacket, checked it covered the set of his gun, and squared a different hat on his head.

He threw saddle purses over his shoulder, checked there was no one outside and opened the back window. 'Wish me luck, gal.'

And he was gone.

Miss Hester Calloway ran the town's millinery store. Business was doing very well and she had plans to expand. Trouble was, her plans exceeded her present funds so she had approached Mr Fisk at the bank for a loan and he had fixed an appointment for her to come and discuss the matter. What she didn't realize was that Mr Fisk had designs on her that went beyond the financial and that was why he had arranged the meeting after closing hours.

She looked at the clock. She would have closed up by now and been on her way if there hadn't been a particularly choosy customer still on the premises. Hester wanted to make her excuses but the customer was a regular big spender, not to be dismissed hurriedly.

Hester looked at the clock as it ticked noisily towards four and unconsciously drummed her fingers on the counter as the lady hummed-and-aahed over the display.

Meanwhile, Jake circuited the town along the back lines until he got to the rear of the saloon just up from the bank and stashed his large saddle purses behind some beer casks. He walked along the avenue between the two buildings and nonchalantly strolled towards the bank. There were a few townsfolk but none paid him any attention.

Inside the bank he raised his bandanna over his face. He was in luck – there were no customers. The two bankmen were occupied with last minute tidying up behind the counter. He turned the pasteboard sign to read CLOSED and pulled his gun.

'This is a stick-up,' he snarled, pulling down the roller blind and throwing the bolts. 'Raise your hands and don't go for the gun in the drawer. That way nobody gets hurt.'

He loped across the open space and pushed through the end gate. 'Both of you into the back room.'

The two white-faced men complied.

'We're making a six-shooter withdrawal here,' Jake snapped. 'That means you cause any trouble – the six-shooter comes into play.'

'You daren't fire your gun,' the older man said. 'It'll be heard. This is a small town in the middle of nowhere. You won't get away.'

'That's for me to worry about. Just close your trap and open the safe.'

'But . . .' Fisk began to say but Jake smashed the gun across his forehead and the older man collapsed in a heap. Jake whirled on the young cashier. 'Like I said, open the safe or you'll get the same.'

'Key's in the front,' the man whispered.

'I'll follow you through,' Jake snapped.

Seconds later the cashier was bent over the safe, swinging open the door. And that was all he knew because Jake's gun came down a second time, this time on the back of his head. He slumped forward, his glasses smashing on the metal sides of the safe.

Jake checked the two men were out for the

count and glanced at the clock. Several minutes past four, so there would be no trouble from customers. That was another risk over.

He slipped out the back door to retrieve his saddle purses. On his return, the older man was coming to, so he slammed him again for good measure.

Now he could take his time. He went to the front and emptied the counter drawers before returning to the back room. He was helping himself to the safe's contents when there came a knock on the glass of the front door.

'Mr Fisk, Mr Fisk.' It was a woman's voice.

He looked at the clock again. Couldn't be a customer. The caller must be coming about some other matter. Maybe she would be persistent, tell somebody that something was odd at the bank. This was unforeseen. He'd have to cut his losses. He took a few more wads and fastened the bags, cursing under his breath at the sight of the mounds of cash still there for the taking. Checking once more that the two men were still immobilized, he headed for the back door. He was just about to open it when there came a knock and the damn voice again.

'Mr Fisk?'

He daren't risk going out the front with the bulging bags over his shoulder. If this woman didn't move her ass, he was trapped.

He pressed his hand against the bandanna to muffle his voice further.

'Yes?'

'Remember our appointment? You said after four.'

He heard groaning as one of the men was coming to. He had to act.

'Come in,' he said, keeping back and opening the door. And he whacked Miss Hester Calloway across the head with his gun.

Thankfully it was still clear out back. He walked swiftly along the backs of the buildings. At the end he reduced his pace to a casual stroll as he crossed the drag, then headed down the southerly back line. Minutes later he had scaled the wall and was back in the hotel. He stashed the bags in one of the valises and started disrobing.

'Come on, gal. Help me get the damn disguise on. All hell's gonna break loose.'

8

It was nearly nightfall when Clay Morgan got back home after another hard day as Junction City's horseless lawman. He called out a few times but no reply signified the house was empty. He stood in contemplation for a moment and rubbed his chin. The stubble reminded him, lighting out so early in the morning he'd not had a chance to shave. He boiled some water. He was just finishing when he heard Liz arrive.

'What are you cleaning yourself up for?' she asked, coming into the kitchen as he was towelling his face.

'Just making myself presentable, is all,' he said, trying to lighten the exchange with a chuckle. 'Can't look like a bum all my life,'

'Huh,' she grunted. 'Seems to me a bum should look like a bum. Ain't honest otherwise.'

He ignored the jibe and packed away his shaving-tackle.

'Suppose you're going drinking,' she sniffed. 'Won't be the first time you've looked for solutions to your problems in the bottom of a bottle.' Clay shook his head. She had a way of making things

79

up, saying the first thing that came into her head
because they sounded good or fitted some view of
the world that she had.

'You know that's not true, Liz. I ain't no
drinker.' He made to kiss her but she pulled away.

'Hell, Lizzy, I'm just trying to be affectionate,'
he said. 'You allus complain when I try to kiss you
when my chin's stubbly.'

'Affectionate?' she snorted. 'You don't know
what the word means. Anyways, you do what you
want, Clay Morgan. I'm going to Eve's for the
evening.'

'Hell, Liz. You spend a lotta time with your
sister these nights.'

'Huh. What is there for me here?'

Soon he was alone in the house. She hadn't
even said goodbye, just noisily slammed the door.

He dropped into an easy-chair and stared at the
embers of the fading fire. His dear Liz had become
one hell of a nag. But it wasn't all her fault – she'd
had her disappointments. She'd had to face their
losing the store, the money it provided, and the
security of its capital value. The mess had worn
him down too. He'd wanted to cut their losses and
move out. That was his reaction: start again some-
place new, a place with prospects. But Liz was
very close to her sister Eve and didn't want to
move too far from her. He could understand her
reluctance to move. He liked his in-laws. With no
remaining family of his own he appreciated the
way they made him feel at home. Should they
move, he would miss them too. Especially their

little boy. Seeing his nephew was a perpetual reminder of how he had wanted kids of his own. But kids hadn't come, one of those things. But now he was glad they had not been blessed. Given their financial straits, children would have been an added burden. Kid? Hell, he couldn't even afford a horse.

So, with one thing and another, he'd become distant in his manner and that, in turn, had put extra strain on their relationship.

And now the loss of his mare. Jeez, he thought to himself as he mulled over these things. When you thought the bad things had finally finished, another bastard comes rolling down the hill.

He remained seated in the darkening house. He was used to sitting alone these days. Liz staying overnight at her sister's was becoming a regular thing. Said she needed a break.

This can't go on, he thought. Time to put some effort into patching things up. But how?

Then he had an idea. He went into the kitchen and made a recce of the stocks. He was no cook but he could make an acceptable chilli, and there was enough food in. That's what he would do. He'd lay the table complete with candles – a flower-vase too – and mosey over to his sister-in-law's, turn on the charm and persuade his missus to return; then treat her to a romantic supper.

He made preliminary preparations, and headed to the other side of town. His sister-in-law looked a little flustered when she saw him at the door.

'Oh, what a pity,' she said when he'd explained his plan. 'I'm sorry, but Liz's retired early.'

'No problem,' he said pertly. 'I'll have a word with her. I think I can talk her round to coming back this evening.'

'I don't think that would be a good idea, Clay. See, er, she has a raging headache.'

He grimaced, let out an 'Oh', then accepted the situation. 'I see. Suppose I'd better leave it at that. Well, be sure to tell her I called. I'll see her in the morning.' He touched his hat. 'Goodnight, Eve.'

'Goodnight, Clay.'

As he strolled back he mulled things over. A headache? Strange. Liz didn't have headaches. Leastways, if she did have one it would be the first. OK, always a first time. He pondered more as he walked. But why go to her sister's, then retire early even if she did have a headache? She could have rested just as easily at home. What if she didn't have a headache? What would be the point of Eve saying she'd had one?

But as he walked home these thoughts were replaced by the other matter eating away at his brain, the problem of acquiring a horse. A couple of days trying to handle his lawman duties without the means to travel around had proved the job to be unworkable. Not relishing a sleepless night in an empty house chewing the matter over, he decided to try to bring the thing to a resolution. He would call on Mr Wilder at home and talk it through man to man. The guy was a banker, for god's sake. What was a hundred bucks with the thousands he'd got in the safe? So he made a detour, to take in Wilder's house.

It was a big place, set back just out of town. There were lights on so he knew the fellow was at home. He pushed through the gate and advanced to the door. He was just about to knock when he heard voices coming from within. It was a warm night and the windows were open. What stopped him in his tracks was the laugh. There was only one person with a laugh like that – Liz. He walked to the side of the house in shadow, and edged along the wall. He came to a window. Jeez!

Liz and Wilder were sitting closely beside each other, each with a drink in hand. As cosy as could be. He fell against the wall, his brain numb as the sight and sounds registered. His immediate reaction was to shoot round to the front door, kick it open and confront them. He imagined the likely scenario. 'What's the matter with you?' she would say. 'Breaking in on two friends having an innocent drink together.' What a jerk he would look. Such action would make things worse.

As the discovery sank in, he leant his back against the wall, his eyes closed. What should he do? He still hadn't come to decision when he became aware of footsteps on the boarded floor inside and of the voices getting fainter. He looked through the window again, just in time to see the couple disappearing upstairs.

Dazed and increasingly sickened, he moved away and trudged slowly homeward. He'd never lied to his wife. Likewise it had never occurred to him that she would lie. Of late things had been difficult between them but he had never lied to her. Like a jackass he'd assumed she didn't lie to him. Back in the house he lay sleepless on the bed. His wife's affections were now obviously and solidly elsewhere. Things fitted into place. Despite the town suffering bad times, Wilder was still well to do. A choice prize for a woman. And what had Clay to offer? Zilch. Hell, what should he do?

Long before morning he had come to decision.

He opened his eyes. Sunlight was pouring in through the undraped window. It took a few seconds for things to come back to him. The short sleep had provided no respite and he was achingly tired – but he knew what he had to do.

He went downstairs, washed and shaved. By the time he had taken a bite to eat, Liz still hadn't returned. It didn't matter. He gathered a few things and stashed them in his warbag. He slung it over his shoulder and walked to the livery stable.

'You going anyplace in the next half an hour, Ike?' he asked.

'No plans. Why?'

Clay dropped his warbag to the hay-strewn floor. 'Can I leave this here for a spell?'

'Sure,' the ostler said and, before the puzzled man could ask what it was all about, Clay had disappeared.

A minute later he was in the bank. There was a woman customer at the counter. He dropped into a seat and watched while the lady completed her business.

'What you come back for?' Wilder asked from behind the grille, suddenly noticing his new visitor.

'Just a chat, is all.'

'We got nothing else to discuss,' the bankman said, 'If it's about that damn horse, we've said it all.'

'All the same,' Clay said, and remained in the chair. When the woman made to leave, the lawman leapt up and opened the door for her.

'Thank you,' she said.

'A pleasure, ma'am,' he said, touching the brim of his hat. When she'd gone he closed the door, threw the bolts, turned the notice to CLOSED and drew down the blind.

'What in tarnation are you doing?' Wilder queried. 'I've only just opened. It ain't closing time,'

'Oh yes, it is,' Clay said, pulling his gun. Before the startled bankman knew it, the sheriff was behind the counter with his pistol levelled.

'It's the time of reckoning,' Clay said, taking the bank manager's gun from the drawer and pushing it into his gunbelt.

'Dunno what you mean.'

'Reckon my business was worth two grand,' Clay went on. 'You remember? The store you burned down?'

'That wasn't my doing, you know that.'

'The hell it wasn't,' Clay snorted, and carried on

with his totalling. 'Two grand. And I need another two hundred dollars, say by way of compensation. So get your ass into the back and take that amount out of your safe – now.'

Wilder eyed the gun. He'd never heard the sheriff talk in these tones before. To him the man had been no more than the weak stooge he'd put in the post as dressing to keep the authorities from sticking their noses in.

'You wouldn't shoot me,' he said. 'You're not the type.'

Clay smiled enigmatically. 'Maybe no, maybe yes. But you know what? You and I ain't gonna know for sure unless you prove awkward.'

'You can't do this.'

Clay chuckled. 'Why not? Who you gonna call? The sheriff?' He chuckled again. Then hardness replaced the smile and he jabbed the gun into the man's fat stomach. 'Now move. And remember, you kindly told me about the other gun, the one in the safe, so don't try anything stupid.'

The apprehensive bankman quickly complied and was soon handing over the stipulated sum.

'What you aiming to do?' he asked as he watched the sheriff peel off $200 and stash the rest in his jacket pocket.

'I'm leaving town.' He patted the bulge in his jacket. 'Just look on this matter as a deal. My part of the bargain is I light out, leaving you a clear field with my missus; I know the way things are between you and Liz. And she's made it plain long since there's nothing between us no more.' The

hardness in his eyes increased. 'And I saw the pair
of you at your house last night'

At the door he paused and holstered his gun.
'You know there's no point in trying anything.' He
took off his badge and threw it on the floor. 'That's
for the next sucker, if'n you can find one.' And he
was gone.

He made a detour to call in at home. Liz still
hadn't returned but it didn't matter any more.
Upstairs he left $1000 in an envelope on her
dressing-table. Whatever he thought of her now,
she still deserved a half-share in the value of their
former store. He took a scent bottle and squirted
it to remind himself of the aroma and old times,
then placed it as a weight on the envelope. He
went through the drawers. There was nothing he
wanted to take save his father's ring. Gold, in the
shape of a coiled snake, he had deemed it too
ornate for everyday wear. He slipped it on his
finger. Then he took a last look round the room.
Now it had come to the crunch he felt no misgivings. It hadn't been a home for years.

Back at the livery stable he walked over to Star
and stroked the animal's neck.

'You said a hundred, Ike,' he reminded the
ostler and took the billfold from his top pocket.
'Said a hundred would stake you to get out of
here. Well, he's a handsome critter. Worth more
than a hundred to me. You've been a good friend,
Ike. There's two hundred. We got a deal?'

'Two hundred? Jeez. Sure thing, Clay.'

The former lawman gave the old man the two

guns from the bank. 'Leave it for a spell, then see
Wilder gets these. He'll feel a mite vulnerable
without them.'

He saddled up.

'Remember,' Ike said as Clay hauled himself up
into the saddle, 'he's a young horse and shows his
spirit once he's on the flat.'

'I'll get used to his ways like he'll get used to
mine.'

'Where you headed?'

'Ike, I ain't being cagey when I say I don't know.
Just ain't made no plans, is all.'

They made their goodbyes. As he pulled out of
town he remembered the feel of Belle beneath
under him. The mother's bloodlines were running
through her son. The same easy movement of
muscle under the silken hide. And the occasional
flick of the magnificent head, just the way his ma
used to. And the young stallion's walk flowed into
a trot and then a gallop in the same seamless way.

A quarter-hour later Clay Morgan was well on
his way. Ahead, he didn't know what – but at least
the hope of a new life. One thing he did know: a
whole mess of troubles lay behind him. And also
behind him lay a nowhere place called Junction
City.

He smiled at the irony. So insignificant a place
in fact, it wasn't even a one-horse town any more.

9

Booked into a hotel, Jake was going through their supplies.

'Hey, kid, we're low on coffee and sugar.' He peeled some bills off his wad and handed them to her. 'Haul your pretty ass into town and buy some.'

'This pretty ass is sore from a day's riding and wants to rest on something soft for a spell.'

The look in Jake's eyes was not exactly pleasant. 'Don't answer back, woman.'

She shrugged in acquiescence and headed for the door. A little later, having made her purchases, Fran stepped out of the grocery store. She paused on the boardwalk, thought of the man to whom she was returning, and deliberately walked away from the hotel. Even though she really wanted to rest, she would take the opportunity to explore the town. The longer she was out of that man's company the better.

From the blacksmith's at one end of town came the clang of metal against metal. From the other, the sound of cowpunchers noisily going about their business in cattle pens. As she negotiated passage between passers-by she noticed handbills tacked to uprights along the way. Eventually she stopped to read one.

The bulk was in classy print and read: DRAMATIC READINGS by the celebrated actor MR ROYSTON LOXLEY, Confidante of Mr Charles Dickens, who will be reading from the esteemed works of his Renowned Colleague along with a selection of readings from the renowned works of Messrs Longfellow, Hawthorne and Shakespeare.

Added in large handwriting below the print was: *Tonight at the Silver Star Hotel 7 p m.*

Back in the hotel she relayed her observation to Jake and expressed an interest in going. 'A confidante of Charles Dickens, no less,' she added excitedly.

'Who the hell's he?' Jake responded.

'Only just about the most famous writer in the whole wide world.'

'Huh, pen-pushers! As useful as teats on a boar. Not for the likes of you and me, kid.'

She dropped disconsolately into a chair. 'Not for you, you mean. All we ever do is ride, sit in saloons and knock banks off. We never do what I want to do.'

'Why the interest, anyhow?'

She took the book from the dressing-table. 'Look. I'm reading one of his very books now.'

'What started you off with all that caper anyhows?'

'I read one of Dickens's books once at school.'

'Huh, school. Them schoolteachers, they're as useless as pen-pushers.'

'Well, that book was one of the best things I've ever read.'

He dismissed the conversation. 'Listen, when we've got some food in our bellies, we're gonna mosey around, check out the town's saloon life.'

'That's all we ever do.'

He grunted in frustration. 'OK, kid. But you go by yourself.'

'Ain't right for a lady to go out at night in a strange town unescorted. Not proper.'

Jake snorted. 'Oh, so you're a lady now, are you? Where did you get a damn fool idea like that?' Then: 'I've told you, kid. If you want to go to a boring shindig like that, you go by yourself.'

The Silver Star hotel was one of the more genteel lodging establishments in town. The event was being held in a hall just off the hotel lobby and chairs had been arranged facing a rostrum on a small stage. She paid her dollar and took a seat at the front and looked around. Slowly people drifted in, mainly groups of elderly women.

Many of them nodded politely to her. She thought of Jake, quaffing his liquor in some smoky saloon, looking for some suckers to gyp at cards, and she was glad she had come unescorted. He would be out of place here anyway. Oh yes, he could be suave and smooth when it profited him. But it was all on the surface.

A banjo clock on the wall ticked very slowly

towards seven; then, when the room was about three-quarters full, the chattering fell away and Fran turned to see a couple of men approaching down the aisle.

Getting to the stage, one of the men, an elderly fellow in a fancy vest, raised his hands to subdue the last of the whispering. Then, saying how happy they were to have someone of the stature of Mr Royston Loxley visiting their humble town, he raised his hand in invitation for their visitor to take the rostrum.

The celebrity made a striking figure. In evening dress with a starched shirt he was a good six feet in height. But more than that – she had never seen a man more handsome. Eyes wide, she watched as he took an ornate watch from his pocket, unclipped it from its chain and laid it before him on the rostrum. The capturing of her heart was complete when he began to speak. Deep, rich tones. And the enunciation had a clarity she had never heard before in a voice – the way she imagined an English aristocrat would speak.

For a while he talked of his friend Charles Dickens, describing the famous author's life in London and extolling the virtues of his books. Then he delivered the advertised selections: scenes from books, poems and extracts from plays. Some he read from the page, others he delivered extempore, strolling round the stage in an acting fashion.

Fran was completely captivated.

After the conclusion of the performance, she joined the throng of women clustered around the great man. There were many questions and then, one by one, they made their goodbyes until eventually Fran was alone with the actor. When she thanked him and made to leave, he stayed her.

'Do you have to rush away, my dear?' he asked.

She thought of the empty hotel room that awaited her.

'Not immediately.'

'Then let me invite you for a quiet drink. It's so rare for me to find myself in the company of someone as refined yet so young and delectable as yourself. I can tell by the questions you asked, you have read something of the works of Mr Dickens. Nothing untoward, you understand.' He looked around. 'I trust they have some civilized libations such as port or sherry in this establishment.'

Port? Sherry? These were drinks she'd never heard of. Shortly, with small fluted glasses of sherry before them, they were seated in a secluded part of the foyer.

'Do you really know Charles Dickens?' she asked. 'I mean, are you really a friend of his?'

He smiled. 'I must admit, my dear, that stuff on the handbills is a slight exaggeration. What we who tread the boards call poetic licence.' He noted the look of disappointment that had swept over her face. 'Only an exaggeration, mark you. I did meet him once and, indeed, exchanged some words with the great man himself.'

'In London?'

'No, it was in New York. He was touring the US coast to coast, doing readings from his works. You must have heard about the tour. It was very successful and was publicized across the nation.'

She shook her head.

'Well,' he went on, 'I was a member of a company of actors. We had just had a good run in New York, but before we, the cast, received our final payment the manager disappeared with all the takings. I was not only completely devoid of finances but there were no other opportunities in other productions at that time. It was seeing Mr Dickens give one of his reading sessions that gave me the idea. And I've been doing it ever since. Of course I don't pull crowds of the same magnitude as the master, but it keeps the proverbial wolf from the door.'

'And a magnificent job you do of it too.'

'Thank you, my dear.'

They talked for a long time during which he asked as many questions as she did. She told him something of her life, careful to omit any mention of criminal activity, explaining that she was assistant to a travelling businessman. But she couldn't hide the fact that she was unhappy in her circumstances, and not emotionally attached to her companion.

When she said, 'You know, it's always been a dream of mine to be an actress,' he studied her silently for a while. Then he opened one of his books and invited her to read a passage.

'I have a proposal,' he said when she had

finished. 'Listening to you perform, I wonder: would you deign to be *my* assistant? It would be an advantage on both sides. For my part, your presence would add a touch of glamour to the proceedings. You can read well and there's nothing wrong with your diction that a little coaching wouldn't improve.'

'You mean it?'

'Of course I do. With you as an added attraction I can see the proceeds rising and you would be remunerated accordingly. Everything would be above board. Separate hotel rooms, naturally.'

'I don't think Jake would stand for it.'

'I don't care for doing things underhand but, in the circumstances, do you have to tell him? You're a grown woman.'

'No, I'd have to square it with him. You don't know him, what he is capable of.'

'Well, let me know if you decide positively, my dear. I don't move on for a few days.'

When she got back to her hotelroom, Jake had not returned. She lay in the darkness, exhilarated by the prospect of leaving the ogre to whom she had been shackled and finally living a decent, legitimate life.

10

The train whistling its approach to Monument woke her. Sensing once again the smell of wood smoke, Constance opened her eyes. The long, dragging journey with its monotony of flat plains passing the window had been conducive to much-needed sleep. Even the jolt and jounce of the narrow-gauge tracks had not interfered with her slumber. Refreshed, she disembarked and gave the scene a brief appraisal. She had no intention of lingering. The town no longer held nostalgia for her, just bad memories.

Monument was where she had started life as a domestic servant, only to be expelled from the town and her character slurred after the incident with the young man. A 'bad influence' they had called her. A 'loose woman'. At the time it was a term she didn't understand. Well, as things panned out, that was what she shortly was to become: a 'loose woman'. But there was a difference between being branded a harlot and choosing to be one.

She cast off the memories and left her traps at the railroad depot to walk the short stretch into town. It had changed little. Some new buildings here and there, vaguely familiar faces. But with her powder and paint and quality clothes, there was no fear of her being recognized. Not that it mattered, but she had no wish to be embroiled in useless chitchat.

She took a meal at a restaurant and freshened up. The orphanage was a stretch to the south. She would need transport. She walked to the livery stable that she remembered at the end of town. Outside the wooden building she paused and looked north across the plains to the hills. A dozen miles that way lay the old homestead. Would it be derelict now or would some other family be fighting to scrape a living out of the arid ground? But it was her past – another world – and of no consequence to her now.

She glanced up at the sign over the building – HARRIS LIVERY STABLE – and stepped through the open doors, to be greeted by the smell of horses and hay. A young man was curry-combing one of the animals in a stall. She enquired regarding a conveyance, explaining it would have to be adequate to take another three passengers.

'No problem, ma'am,' he said. 'Got an extra large surrey out back. I'll show it to you if'n you like.' He nodded at the sign 'And that's my name over the door. Ted Harris.' Grabbing a rag, he escorted her out the back door and wiped the seat of the vehicle in an eager-to-please manner.

'And a driver?' she asked.

'Be a pleasure to do so myself, ma'am. I'd appreciate getting the wind in my hair for a spell.'

They struck a deal and he invited her to sit in the shade while he set about preparations. He was just harnessing the horses when there came the sounds of commotion in the street. He raised oblique eyebrows.

'Wonder what that is? Lot of noise for a quiet place like Monument. Excuse me, ma'am.'

Grateful for the opportunity to stretch her legs, she followed the inquisitive lad round to the front. The cause of consternation was a buckboard drawn up in the middle of the thoroughfare, attracting townsfolk from all directions. When she saw what it was carrying for freight – a bloodied human carcass – she pulled a wry face and kept her distance.

But the ostler, with interests that ran the gamut from the prurient to the morbid, pressed forward to investigate.

'What's happened?' he asked of a middle-aged woman whose own degree of curiosity was demonstrated by the way her head craned forward, bobbing eerily like some farmyard hen in search of corn.

'Some stupid critter went moseying into the Grounds.'

Before he'd fully satisfied his own inquisitiveness he remembered he had a customer and returned to her side.

'What befell the poor fellow?' Constance asked.

'Indians.'

'I thought those days were long over.' In her days here there had never been trouble with redmen.

'It's his own fault. Brung it on hisself. Shouldn't have gone near the Grounds. Guess he was a stranger. Mind, there are warning signs posted.'

She knew the Grounds, the local name for the Indians' ancient burial grounds up on Sun Mountain. More of a hill than a mountain, it had formed the backdrop to the homestead of her childhood. The mysterious, eerie place where one should never go. But she had gone. In those days the worst you got was a shooing off if you were espied by any natives. She reminded herself she was supposed to be a stranger and feigned a measure of curiosity.

'What are the Grounds?'

'The local tribe's burial place on Sun Mountain. You know the way the savages leave their dead, up in the air for the buzzards to pick at. No dignity.'

'What about it?'

'A couple of years ago there was a rumour that ore had been found up there and prospectors started coming in from everywheres. Indians didn't cotton to their sacred mountain being dug up and there were some very nasty confrontations with deaths on both sides. Army was called in. Very sacrilegious for a whiteface to be there. In a way the redskins were within their rights because there was already a treaty safeguarding the Grounds. So the territorial authorities along

with the Indian Bureau struck up an extra agreement that not only the Mountain but also all the
land around it would be off limits to whites. Now,
if the redmen catch any whites straying
anywheres near the Grounds they . . .' He nodded
towards the unsightful carcass just visible
between the gathered onlookers. '. . . they do that
to them.'

'What action do the authorities take when the
Indians do that?' she asked.

'Nothing. It'd mean an all-out war and nobody
wants that. There's an agreement and that's that.
It's an uneasy peace but it works – as long as folks
keep to themselves. Whites go where they should-
n't, they get trouble for themselves. The authorities have put enough signs up.'

'How far does the forbidden land extend?'

'Miles in all directions. On this side up to
within a mile of town.' He pointed northward.
'See, if you squint you can just make out the first
of the warning notices.'

That answered one of her earlier questions.
Being right at the foot of Sun Mountain and
within the forbidden zone the old family homestead would have no occupants now. As she gazed
in the direction that the young man pointed, she
momentarily had an image of the old place. The
little sod-house with the vegetable patch and
water-well out front. Certainly derelict now,
maybe even just a bare ruin.

The two observed the proceedings until the
body was being carried into the funeral parlour,

then they returned to the back of the livery stable and the job in hand.

He looked at the sun as he finished harnessing the horses. 'Take about an hour to get to the orphanage,' he said. And shortly they were heading south along the beaten path in a billowing spume of dust.

The orphanage was situated alongside a steepled church in a small hamlet. The building itself was quite substantial, an imposing two-storey affair with set-back portico and large bay windows, not the ramshackle place she'd expected. Her driver pulled the surrey in near the door and she alighted.

She pulled the bell and by the time the door was finally answered half a dozen young heads had appeared at windows.

'Yes?' The question came from an elderly woman shrouded in a floor-length black dress. She appraised the caller in a considered up-and-down movement as she spoke.

'The name's Constance Shaw.'

The wizened neck stretched out of the high white-lace collar as she inspected the surrey over Constance's shoulder. 'I don't recognize you but the name is familiar.'

'It should be. I pay for my sisters to live here.'

The woman stiffened. 'What can I do for you?'

'I've come to collect them.'

'You'd better come in. I'll call the Reverend.'

Constance was shown into a parlour and she

took the time to look over the room while the woman went on her errand. The massive furniture was highly polished. Thick carpets cushioned her feet. Not the accoutrements associated with the poor church mice of folklore.

Eventually a black-garbed man of the same age made an appearance.

'The Reverend Thackeray at your service, ma'am. Would you like to sit down?'

'Better still – I'd like to see my sisters,'

'I am afraid that is not possible. They are no longer with us.'

'Not with you? Why was I not informed? I'm still sending payments. Substantial payments.'

'Yes,' he faltered. 'I am afraid we have been rather dilatory in informing you. We are planning to send you a communication.' He pointed to a roll-top desk. 'In fact, I am in the process of drafting a letter to you.'

'Well, where are the girls?'

The man ignored her question and cleared his throat importantly. 'While it is relatively easy to find employment for our young men when they are of age, you must appreciate it is somewhat difficult to find fitting positions for our young ladies. We have to be careful, you understand. We do our best to provide them with the accomplishments requisite for a young lady going out in the world.'

'I'm sure you do a good job. Now, if they are no longer here, where are they?'

He disregarded her again, and continued in

sepulchral tones as though delivering a sermon. 'You see, there are so few occupations a young lady can take up. If we were in a metropolis, the occupation of domestic servant would be a natural channel but out here it is an intractable task to find a family desiring to avail themselves of the services of a maid.'

'I'm losing my patience,' Constance said curtly.

'On the other hand the wilderness is devoid of the female gender and, as a consequence there are many men who are looking for a bride. Of course, we check the credentials of the prospective husbands. We do have to be careful about —'

She cut him short. 'You saying you've set them up as frontier brides?'

'The young ladies in question were of a singular species.'

'You mean pretty?'

'They were of age, legally capable of making up their own minds.'

'My sisters, did they leave together or separately?'

'No, they left on separate occasions.'

Constance finally sat down. 'You get money out of this?'

'Well . . . er . . . there are expenses.'

The thought of her sisters being cast out in such a manner assaulted her mind. But she needed information and didn't want to clam the couple up by giving vent to her anger immediately.

'You'd better give me names and details.'

'A nice man called Mr Harvey,' the woman said. 'Jake Harvey.'

The man summoned the woman to silence with a reproving glance and quickly added, 'Yes, that's right. He was the last one to take responsibility for one of your sisters.'

'And the others?'

'I'm afraid we've had an accident with our records. We don't have details of the others. There are so many young charges passing through our hands, you understand.'

'Well, what can you tell me about this Jake Harvey? Where does he live? Where was he taking her?'

'Can't recall. But, have no fear; he was quite well to do, enough to provide for your sister. Some kind of businessman.'

She pondered on what she had learned, then, 'Talking of finances, you owe me a refund. All the cash I've sent since the girls left.'

'As I said, with our records now incomplete we cannot be precise about the dates of their leaving.'

Constance suddenly stepped toward the man and her parasol shot up sharply between his legs. 'Listen, mister. Never try to jig and jigger.'

The parasol came down before the man could grab it. 'Now, see here,' he snapped, grimacing with the discomfort.

'Now you see here,' she interrupted. 'I'm having full recompense. Figure a grand will cover it.'

'A thousand dollars?' the man said, trying to regain his dignity. 'You must be joking.'

'No joke. If you don't pay up now, I'll take you through the courts. That way the wide world will learn what you're up to.'

The faces of both man and woman noticeably paled and their jaws sagged in consternation. They looked at each other, then the man said. 'We don't hold that much money on the premises.'

'Then you'll accompany me to town this very hour and withdraw it from the bank. I'll be waiting in the surrey.'

As she walked away she could hear the muffled voice of the man berating his companion behind the door. She resumed her seat in the surrey and looked back at the building. It dwarfed the small church beside it, prompting the question in her mind which building was the appendage of which. It was clear the church was there merely to confer respectability on the business conducted by the old hornswogglers.

Back in Monument, after she'd got her money, she booked in at the Republic hotel. Then she toured the saloons asking about Jake Harvey. Men of whom she made enquiries eyed her with the look reserved for strangers but came up with nothing. After an unfruitful hour she returned to the hotel and was walking through the saloon section on her way to the stairs when a drinker raised his hand.

'Excuse me, ma'am, I hear you're asking after Jake Harvey.'

She stopped and looked in the direction of the

speaker, a hairy man with eyebrows that met above his nose.

'Yes,' she responded querulously.

'What do you want to know?'

She looked around and took a seat across the table from him. 'Anything.'

'Is this something to do with the law?' His question was presented in conspiratorially low tones. 'He wanted or something?'

'No, it's family business.'

He nodded. 'What's it worth?'

'Christ, is everybody in this place on the make? The man shrugged.

'OK,' she conceded. 'Depends what you got.'

'I got a description.'

She opened her purse and put a couple of bills on the table.

'Clean-cut feller,' the man said. 'Rides a sorrel.'

'You know him?'

'No. But figure he comes from way down south the way he talks.'

'Well, if you don't know him you must have some reason for remembering his name and details.'

'Seed him a few times is all. Here in Monument.'

'How many times?'

'Figure three times.'

'How come you can be so precise?'

'I'm a handyman by trade, ma'am. Do repairs, gardening and such for the Reverend and his missus over at the orphanage. Seen your Mr

Harvey visiting there. Came three times. Was
close enough to get his name. Or at least what he
said was his name.' He lapsed into silence as she
looked at him.

'Carry on,' she prompted. Still silence.

She unravelled a couple more bills which he
accepted, prompting him to add, 'He gives the
name of Harvey, but that's not his name. It's Jake
all right, but his second name is Bridger.'

'How do you know that?'

'Because someone called him Bridger, acciden-
tal like. Somebody passing through who knew
him from elsewheres. When the feller used that
name your friend looked around like a disturbed
rattler, and hissed "Name's Harvey. Jake Harvey".
So, figure his real name's Bridger.'

'OK, his real name's Bridger. You saw him take
a girl from the orphanage?'

The man chuckled. 'One? He took three, one
each time he came.'

For a moment Constance was lost for words.
Then, 'Do you remember when?'

'Last time was a few months back. Afore that a
couple of times spread over the last year.'

'The Reverend and his missus, they running
some kind of a business over there?'

'They off-load the kids when they're growed up.
Get a lotta guys wanting brides. Figure the old
couple take money for the girls. Hell, everybody's
gotta make a living. Guess it works out cheaper
for the fellers too – cheaper than getting one from
one of them high-falutin New York mail-order

companies. 'Sides they can see what they're getting afore they purchase.'

'This Bridger took three? Why would one man want three?'

The fellow chuckled. 'Mebbe he's a Saint. Out in Utah a man can have as many wives as he can handle.'

'Know anything else about him?'

'No. Saving the direction he rode out.'

'Which way?'

The man fingered his money. 'You ain't paid enough, Ma'am.'

She passed another couple of bills across.

'Came up along the southern trail. Rode back that way.'

'That's all you know?'

'Yeah.'

She nodded. 'Thanks.'

He rolled up the bills and pushed them into his vest pocket. 'Oh, and I can tell you something else for free. He's shy of a finger. Pinkie on his left hand. Usually wears a glove to cover it, but I noticed it once when he took the glove off to fix the buckles on his saddlebag.'

'You sure see a lot for a gardener.'

'It pays a man to keep his eyes open.' He patted the new bulge in his vest pocket. 'Like now.'

She nodded, laying her enigmatic smile on him.

'Rule of life, ma'am. Appearances can be deceptive. I ain't the see-nothin'-hear-nothin' odd job man folks take me for. Your Mr Harvey, or should I say, Bridger, ain't quite the man he seems either.' He gave her his own version of a smile. 'Just like you ain't the innocent tea-drinking drawing-room lady you give out to be.'

She rose and slipped him another couple of bills. 'If you can remember anything else I'm booked in at the Republic.'

In her room she dropped in a chair and gave thought to what she had learned. Something smelled about the set-up. She dismissed the notion of this Bridger being a Mormon. The only thing she could think of was the sidewinder was supplying a cathouse. She cringed at the notion. One hooker in the family was bad enough but four – their poor old ma would be spinning in her grave.

There was only one thing to do: find out where he had taken them. It was a needle in a haystack job but there was nothing else for it. Worse, she had to find the haystack first. The one virtue to the whole shebang: she had enough money to finance some kind of search. She dismissed consideration of what she would do when the cash ran out.

She began to remove her formal attire before the mirror. Her powder had blown off and her lip-paint was smudged. After taking off her bonnet she unpinned her hair and shook it free. Running her fingers through it she could feel trail-dust and grit.

She appraised her reflection. She would have to change her garb to something more fitting to the outdoor. And she'd need her own means of travel.

*

The next day, dressed in shirt and Levis, she went looking for a horse. Although not a practised rider, she'd learned the rudiments of riding on her father's old mare. After purchasing a grey along with accoutrements and a packhorse she bought a small rifle and saddle boot. A woman travelling alone across the wilderness would need some kind of protection.

11

The trail passed a hill that sloped against the sun. Jake led the way up the grade to a clutch of trees and the couple dismounted to take advantage of the shade. He growled an instruction to his companion to get the canteen, then cupped his hands so that she could fill them with water.

When they had watered the horses and taken a swig themselves they relaxed under a tree. Jake lit a cigarette and scanned the terrain, a permanent glower in his eyes. Ahead a trail crossed the one they were on.

Fran followed his gaze. 'How far to the next town?' she asked.

'How the crap should I know? Never been in these parts before.' Then he grunted, 'Another hour's ride. Two mebbe.' After that they didn't speak. Neither had spoken much for two days. Save for Jake muttering 'Ten grand.' Over and over he had muttered it. With an interspersing of expletives. And variants such as 'Must have been at least ten grand.'

Two days since they had left the last town in one mother of a hurry. Ever since then Jake had been like a bear with a sore head and she'd known better than antagonize him with things like conversation. It was understandable. They had left so fast he hadn't been able to get up to their hotel room to collect his loot before leaving. He hadn't told her why the haste. She just assumed that somebody had recognized him. After all, there was a passel of wanted posters on him. And it had happened before. That was one of the reasons he kept on the move. And why he needed the cover of a woman during his heists. Figured a man-and-woman couple looked less suspicious. Seemed to work.

She lay back, closed her eyes and listened to the insects buzzing in the heat. In the early days she had been happy to be in the company of the handsome Jake. He had introduced her to the world, taught her things. He was the first man who had taken her to his bed and he had taught her things there too. There had been fine clothes. He had a way of making a woman feel special. But in time the scales had fallen from her once-innocent eyes and she realized the charm was superficial. Underneath there was something cold. And the finery, the first store-bought clothes she had ever had, were only dressing for the various roles he had her play.

'Hello, we got company,' he said after a while. She opened her eyes to see him squinting into the distance. She followed the direction of his scrutiny and saw a lone figure coming along the cross trail. Eventually the rider angled into the long-grass scrub, heading their way.

'He can't have seen us yet,' Jake said. 'I'll hide the horses and take cover.'

'What you gonna do?'

'Take him for whatever he's got.'

'He's just a trail bum.'

'We're damn broke, you knuckleheaded female. That's why. Now, you attract him up here where I can get a good look at him.'

'How do I do that?'

'Hell, woman,' he snapped, standing up and taking their horses' reins. 'Wave, call, look distressed. If he's a Good Samaritan he'll oblige.'

'What shall I say?'

'Say you got throwed by your horse. But get him close so I can get the drop on him. Make believe you're injured. That'll take his concentration.'

Clay Morgan's horse cleared the long grass, then footed easily along the worn trail. He'd gone a few hundred yards when he heard a shout. He reined in and turned in the saddle. Up near a stand of trees a girl was waving. He glanced around, saw no one else and gigged his horse up the incline.

'What's happened, ma'am?'

'I fell from my horse.' She was rubbing her arm.

He dismounted. 'You OK?'

'Yes. Bruised maybe but no bones broken.'

'Where's your horse?'

'Made off over the ridge yonder. It happened down there on the trail. I was coming up here to look for him when I saw you.'

'Well, you stay here, ma'am. I'll mosey up to the

ridge and have a scout around, see if I can spot him.'

He turned his back and was about to put his foot in the stirrup when a voice boomed, 'Don't bother, pilgrim. Put your hands in the air and stand away from the horse.'

He started to turn but something prodded against his spine. 'No, pal, don't turn round. Now take it easy while I relieve you of your gun.'

But that's as far as the conversation went because something crashed against his skull. He pitched forward against his horse, tried to get a hold of the saddle but the strength had gone from his limbs. He distantly made out the girl saying 'I'm sorry, mister,' before awareness deserted him.

'Hell,' Jake snarled as Clay's disturbed horse shot off. 'We lost the horse. Damn, good piece of horseflesh. That and the saddle would have fetched a fair piece of change.' He checked the man was out and took his gun. 'Anyways, why the hell did you say sorry?' he said as he started going through the man's pockets.

'You didn't have to hit him.'

'Better he didn't see me.'

'Oh, it's OK for him to see me, is it?'

'That was unavoidable. Now don't sass me, woman.'

Clay came to with a head that felt like it was a tom-tom being played by some frenzied Indian. He staggered to his feet and rubbed the back of his skull. Jeez, it was tender. He explored his pockets. They were empty. His pa's ring had been wrenched from his finger. No horse either. He dragged his feet over to a tree and slipped down, back against the trunk. Eventually he was composed enough to move. He heavy-footed down the grade and paused on the trail. He was in unknown territory. He contemplated his situation for a spell. Hell, he didn't even know how far to the next town.

The day was closing in as the two made their way along the trail.

'Hey, I just remembered.' Jake said suddenly, swinging round in his saddle to look at the girl. 'What was that stuff about you saying sorry to that sucker back there?'

'What are you talking about?'

'You said sorry to the bozo. What the hell was that about?'

'He was just an ordinary feller, Jake. Maybe just a plain cowhand or something.'

'So?'

'Fleecing rich folks is one thing but working over an everyday working guy – that's something else. Might have a wife and kids. Even if he don't, he was just a regular joe going about his business.'

'Regular joe? Huh! In our game no sucker is too small. 'Sides, we're broke.' He turned to face the way ahead, muttering, 'Dunno what's getting into you lately, gal.'

She let the conversation die for a while, then

said. 'And you didn't have to lay him out.'

'Hell, you sure got some burr in your britches. And yes. I did have to drop him. Best he didn't see me.' He reined in, dismounted. He ground-hitched his horse, rubbed his backside and stretched. He took out a cigarette and lit it. 'You know what? You're getting a mite sassy, gal.' He said it with a growl. Fran knew the signs and kept her counsel.

She dismounted and sat on the grass some feet away, watching him. He pulled a timepiece from his vest pocket and checked the time. Fran's face blanched. She recognized the watch. Without speaking she rose, advanced towards him and, before he could stop her, she had wrenched the thing from his hand. 'This was Royston Loxley's!'

She thrust it towards him. 'What does it mean?'

Jake just cackled.

'What did you do to him?' she screamed.

He cackled louder. 'Let's say he ain't gonna be spewing out his claptrap no more.'

'You killed him?' She went for his face with her nails. 'You didn't have to kill him!'

He grabbed her wrists and whirled her sideways so she fell to the ground. 'Why did you think we had to leave town in such a hurry, you stupid bitch?'

She had known something was wrong because she'd been passing time in a saloon when he'd he come in and bustled her off to the horses, giving no more explanation than that they had to get out pronto. Everything fell into place now. She had

told him she wanted to join up with the actor.
Jake had been angry at the thought, told her it
wasn't going to happen. But after the initial burst
of temper she'd thought that had been the end of
it. She should have known better. Jake could hold
a long grudge.

'You murderer!' she screamed and leapt at him
once more. He felled her with one sledgehammer
blow to her delicate jaw.

Semi-conscious, she could discern his shape
looking over her. She could vaguely make sense of
the words. Something like 'It's all your fault, you
cow. If it wasn't for you I wouldn't be in this pig's
mess. Damn your eyes. I'm making my way without you from now on. You've never been no use.
Like your damn sisters. Nothing but trouble.'

Mention of her sisters kick-started her senses.

'Is this way you treated Meg and Bess?' she
murmured. 'Did you smack them around too?
Make you feel a big tough guy, does it, beating up
on women? Did you leave them at the trailside
too?'

At that, he got real close. 'Never know when to
shut up, do you? Well, this is the big *adios*, gal.
Just to remind you what'll happen to you if you go
mouthing off to the law about me —'

And the next blow knocked her out completely.

Clay had walked for maybe half an hour. Many
times he had cursed himself for not wearing his
handgun. He might have stood a chance. In toting
his gun-belt on his horse while travelling in the

middle of nowhere, he had acted like a greenhorn. In fact like a storekeeper. Which was what he was. Anyways, he had lost his horse, his money and his gun. His one consolation was that he had split the money into two. spending money in his jacket pocket, the bulk packed away on his horse. So although he himself had lost it all, at least the bushwhacker hadn't got his mangy hands on the main stash in the saddlebag. A small consolation.

So much for starting a new life. And what a new life. These were his thoughts when he turned a bend in the trail and to his amazement saw Star quietly grazing – like nothing had happened. His spirits soared. He stopped in his tracks, at first not believing his eyes. Then he began to walk cautiously forward, whispering the animal's name. The horse looked up as he neared, flicked his tail, then continued grazing as though this kind of escapade was a daily occurrence.

Clay took the bridle and patted the horse's neck. 'Why didn't you tell me you were hungry, you son-of-a-gun?'

He checked out the caparisons. Nothing had been touched. As he unpacked his gun-belt and slung it around his hips, his spirits hit a new peak. The cost of the escapade had now fallen to around two hundred dollars and a bump on the head. He could live with that. But what stuck in his craw was the varmint taking his pa's ring.

A mile further on he had another surprise. As soon as he saw the figure he recognized it as that of the girl who had acted as bait in jumping him!

He reined in and pulled his gun, scanning the environs as he did so. He couldn't see her accomplice – but he was taking no chances. He took refuge behind a tree and maintained his vigil. She was trudging along the trail, seemingly alone. Might be another one of their decoy tricks. He gigged his horse up a grade and made his way slowly along a ridge in the same direction. He waited until she was well in the open. That way there was no chance of being jumped again. Keeping a weather-eye open and gun in hand he made his way down.

'Hold on there, missy,' he said as he neared. She turned, started when she recognized him, then slumped on the grass beside the trail. He noted she had no weapon. Glanced around, still couldn't see the man. 'Where's your confederate?' he snapped, pulling short.

'Long gone.'

'So you say.' As he spoke he kept up his watch on the full compass. 'This another one of your tricks?'

She indicated her swollen lip. 'Does this look like a trick?'

He noted the bloodied mouth and dark bruise on her cheekbone. He hadn't taken too much stock of her features first time round, but he recalled enough to know these were new additions.

'So, what happened?'

She dropped her eyes to the ground. 'We had words. He lit out.'

'Well, what d'you know? No honour amongst thieves.'

She didn't answer, just watched as he dismounted on the other side of the trail and ground-hitched his horse.

'Glad to see you've got your horse back,' she said, and resumed staring blankly at the dust between her feet.

'Gee, it sure is a comfort to hear you say so,' he sneered. 'No thanks to you, missy. Anyways, never mind that. We got some things to hash over.'

'What you gonna do?'

'You got any of the stuff from my pockets?'

'No. Jake's got it.'

'So his name's Jake. Jake who?'

'You gonna turn me over to the law?'

He grunted: 'Huh.' It was a humourless grunt. 'Law? I am the law.'

That caused her to look up again. Then she hissed some indecipherable expletive, shaking her head, and looked back at the ground.

'You really the law?'

'Well, I was,' he elaborated. 'Till a short spell back.'

'How come you're not now?'

'Took early retirement. Not that it's any of your business. Anyways, back to the subject, I want some names. His, yours.'

She played dumb.

'Listen, missy. I got two options. I can take you in to the next town and press charges at the law office. Or I can leave you here and when I get there, notify the sheriff myself and he'll come out a-looking. Meantimes you'll have to fend for yourself out here. Either way you've got trouble and you're gonna have to talk. Might as well tell me what I want to know.'

'Oh, what the hell,' she began; then answered all his questions.

'So he beat up on you 'cos you'd decided to split?' he said when she'd finished. She nodded. She hadn't told him about the killing.

'And you've really finished with him?'

'Mister, it was a terrible life.'

He thought on it. 'Tell you what I'm gonna do. I said I had two options. Well, there's a third. Assuming you're telling the truth – that is until you give me cause to think otherwise – I'm gonna make you an offer. I take you to the next town but I don't turn you in. I want to nail the critter myself. If I can get my mitts on him first I stand a chance of getting my money back – and my old man's ring. But I don't know what the guy looks like so I'll need your co-operation.'

'Jake's got a nasty side to him. Figure he'd kill me if he knew I fingered him.'

'Well, we don't have to let Jake know it's you doing the fingering.'

'What happens to me then? You turn me in?'

'That's a bridge we'd have to cross when we come to it. But if you co-operate like I'm suggesting and help me out, you'll have me on your side.'

'OK, mister. Seems like a good enough way to get this business behind me. It's a bargain.'

'Fine. But remember I'm gonna be watching you all the way.'

12

The country was vast, but if Constance made some assumptions about her quarry the problem was less intractable. This Jake Bridger, whatever his purpose, was not to know he was being sought so would travel in an uncomplicated manner. He had no reason to go this way, that, and double back to confound pursuers. Secondly, if she assumed he had no reason to leave the beaten track, then she could restrict her search to the towns and settlements on the map.

It took her four hours to reach the next town. By the time her horse was plodding up the main drag every muscle in her body groaned. She had heard the term 'saddle-weary' used many times; now she knew what it meant. All thoughts of her quest had left her mind and it was all she could do to get the animals fixed up in a livery stable, book into a hotel and collapse onto a soft, soft bed.

As the days passed she became more horse-wise, her backside hardened to the saddle and her limbs ached less and less. She quickly found herself to be the object of unwanted attentions from men wherever she went. A lone female, she

would be looked at curiously by woman-hungry
bozos but she would dismiss them brusquely. Her
early adult years had been spent attracting men.
Now she wore heavy shirt and jacket to mask her
shapeliness, and baggy Levis to defeminise her
figure. Eventually she bought a poncho from a
'breed. Not only was it practical but it detracted
even more from her femininity. In a wild and
lonely country, deficient in law and order and civilized behaviour, you didn't put your goods on obvious display. Without powder and paint, her face
soon became tanned and her skin dried and
flaked. Without access to her daily bath she took
on an odour, strange and abhorrently noticeable
to her own nostrils – but unremarked by the rest
of the smelly community. Her hair became permanently dusty and matted.

Meanwhile Clay and Fran, in pursuit of the same
goal, were working on extra information. They
knew in which direction Bridger had ridden. They
also knew, at least at the moment, that he was
without a female accomplice. They also knew he
was broke.

'He's not going to chance any stick-ups,' Fran
deduced as the pair of them pondered on a map of
the territory which Clay had bought. 'And he's
only got one way of making money by himself.
Card-sharping. He's used to big money so he won't
bother with small towns.' She drew her finger
across the map in the direction their quarry had
last been heading. 'So we make some enquiries,

find out where the big money games are, and check 'em out one by one.'

'Nothing to it,' Clay said.

Fran looked at him. 'Nothing to it? You must be joking.'

Clay grinned. 'I was.'

Constance journeyed through the summer heat. She would fetch up in a town and make rest her first priority. Moseying through the streets she would merely watch and listen. Only when she was about to leave a town would she ask questions: at the saloons, the general stores, and finally the law office, where incumbents would look at her quizzically. Sometimes she would hear of some travelling couple, but further questioning would reveal that something didn't fit in the description. Folks reacted variously. Some were suspicious, reticent and unhelpful. Others loved to talk. Yet others would fix on turning the situation to their advantage and try to sell her something. And, of course, there were always those who would want to buy something from her.

Whenever possible she would make her enquiries of women rather than men. The women, through their general-store gossiping, would know as much, if not more, than the menfolk about the town's comings and goings. But nothing tangible materialized.

This was the first time she'd travelled since she'd first left home. But there was no homesickness; she realized she didn't fit any place. She was hit by a recurring nightmare in which her money was all used up and she still hadn't found her sisters. As time passed the dream visited her with increasing frequency. When she saw her money running through her fingers like water, she learned some basic economics. It was much cheaper to make your own coffee. Jerky or a pan of beans was cheaper than restaurant meals. While the weather kept fine it was cheaper to bed out in the open, but that was one economy she didn't chance too often.

From time to time, the comprehension of the enormity and seeming hopelessness of her task overwhelmed her. She contemplated taking on help. She knew there were agencies that specialized in that kind of thing. She could employ some experienced investigator to do the tiring riding and legwork. But the prospect of the expense quickly ruled that out. During times of frustration – when there seemed no hope ahead – she would contemplate the unthinkable: giving up. But then her innate stubbornness would reassert itself. The only thing was to press on. She had no plans to go home. She had no home.

By the end of the summer she was weaker and disheartened. She remained longer in each town. Her cross-country progress snailed up, with short hauls and long rest-ups between.

Had her long, dogged search been enough? In terms of time and effort the answer would be yes. But in terms of results the answer would be no. With diminished funds her search was becoming less practicable, taking its toll on her physical and financial resources. And her horse and pack pony were showing signs of exhaustion. With winter in sight her implacability was hard hit.

Summoning up some vestiges of resolution, she bought a new horse and mule, replenished her packs and once more headed out – with renewed determination to look for a woman and a man with a missing finger.

Then her luck changed.

She walked the town, grateful for the chance to stretch her legs. She passed the lights of stores, occasionally pausing to give the displayed goods a look. Beautiful clothes and hats, merchandise she had forgotten the feel of. She lingered at a corner and watched the passing traffic. Freight wagons coming in after a long haul; buckboards laden with newly purchased stuff, leaving for distant homesteads; riders coming in for a night on the town. She listened to the noise, the joshing, the music coming from saloons.

She was about to cross the street when, amongst the various musics melding into one cacophony, she detected the wheezing notes of an accordion coming from a saloon behind her. And for a brief moment she felt the pangs of nostalgia, the first she had felt for a long time. It was the warmth of that nostalgia that tempted her through the batwings. The place was not crowded: a few drinkers, a little action around the black-jack table; at the side of a curtained stage a young fellow in vest and derby hat, one arm swinging the bellows of a squeezebox while the hand of the other fingered the keyboard.

She bought a drink and remained at the bar. She rebuffed a couple of advances, and leaned on the counter, absorbing the atmosphere. Her new life was so different. With most of her time spent in the saddle alone she now appreciated the noise of folk, talking, having a good time.

As she stood there with her thoughts, the music was becoming increasingly familiar and she began to listen more attentively. The familiarity lay in the little curlicues of notes the squeezebox player threw in to decorate the tune. Pa had used to do that. And Meg had learnt the habit from him. Intrigued she approached the stage. Up close she couldn't believe it. The fellow playing the squeezebox wasn't a fellow at all.

'Meg!'

The accordion wheezed discordantly into silence. 'Connie!'

Annoyed at the abrupt ceasing of music, the proprietor made his way across.

'Can I sit out for a spell, Joe?' the player said. 'This here's my sister. My long lost sister.'

They hugged, there were tears. Then they went behind the curtains for privacy and histories were exchanged. Bess had been the first one to be purchased by Jake. Then a season on he had turned up at the orphanage and bought Meg. When she couldn't take any more of his beatings she had lit out. During her time with Jake she had got a good idea of where he had dumped Bess. So she had gone looking for her, supporting herself by playing squeezebox in saloons. In time she had found her elder sister but there was an element of tragedy. She learned that Bess hadn't been long with the critter before she had become pregnant. As soon as he learned of her condition he dumped her. However, she not only lost the baby but the troubled birth had turned her a little simple-minded. Doctor had said something about blood-poisoning.

'That's another nail in the bastard's coffin,' Connie hissed.

'Be that as it may,' Meg said. 'Let me take you to what we call home.' And she took Connie to the shack on the outskirts of town where she and Bess lived. There were more tears and hugs.

'How do you survive?' Connie asked.

'The squeezebox provides enough dollars to keep food in our bellies and a roof over our heads.'

'Some roof,' said Connie looking askance at the accommodation. 'Well, these days are over. No Shaw girl is going to live like this while I can help it. First off, I'll book us into a hotel in town. We'll have a slap-up meal. Then tomorrow we'll start talking about the future.'

The next day the three girls were sitting on plush finery in the town's best hotel. They'd all luxuri-ated in a hot tub and covered themselves in sweet-smelling potions. Connie had decked her sisters out in new clothing.

'We've two aims,' Connie was saying. 'Our main priority is to find Fran. Get her out of whatever mess she's in. Second, we're gonna nail this Bridger critter once and for all. God knows how we're gonna trace him. But one thing's for sure, it's gonna need a heap of travelling. How you gonna be, Bess? Can you handle travel?'

Bess touched her head with her finger. 'I'm not a cripple, Connie. And I ain't stupid. Just a little slow is all. Sure I can handle travel.'

'Good.'

'But how do we set about tracking Fran?' Meg asked.

'Fran is with Bridger or, if he's dumped her, she'll be somewhere along his backtrail. So either way, our only bet is tracking Bridger.'

'That's a needle in a haystack.'

Connie smiled. 'You were a needle in a haystack. I found you.' Then: 'We've got some advantages. We know the way he works, pulling off jobs in conjunction with a woman accomplice. There's a chance the law authorities will have a record of that kind of job. Failing them, there's newspaper files.'

13

Fran and Clay got onto his trail quicker than
they'd expected. Their ploy of restricting their
enquiries to towns where there were big money
games paid off. In each town they asked about a
through-rider who came in, made a killing at
cards and rode on. As was the habit of Westerners,
many didn't take kindly to questions from
strangers; but some tried to help out. And, after a
few wild-goose chases, the couple finally got news
of such a man – who also had a missing finger.

The saloon in the little town of St Bernard was
pretty full when they entered. However, they were
tired after a long ride and off-guard, their first
priority simply to get a drink and a rest. They'd
been in the place several minutes when Fran
said, 'That looks like him.' She pointed to a card-
game at the back of the room. 'There – the one
with his back to us.'

Clay stiffened, his tired eyes suddenly alert.
'You sure?'

'Not till I see his face. But sure looks like the back
of his ugly neck. And the way the varmint sits.'

'Well, you'll have to identify him,' Clay said. 'Remember, he slugged me from behind so I still don't know what he looks like. Let's mix in with the crowd sitting here while you keep your eye on hilm.'

'What you gonna do?' she asked as they eased themselves into chairs at a crowded table.

'When you're sure it's Bridger, I'll notify the local law. They should co-operate as I'm a fellow officer.'

'You told me you'd resigned.'

'I have. But they don't have to know that. I'll tell 'em they can check with Junction City. They probably won't bother, but even if they try it makes no never-mind – Junction City ain't on the telegraph.'

But all their plans evaporated a few moments later when the object of their attention stood up and walked in their direction. Fran acted instinctively, raising a hand to her mouth.

'My God. It is him!'

Just as instinctively, Clay drew his gun. But it was the wrong thing to do. He was still a green-horn in these situations while Jake was an old hand. There was only one thing to do when seeing the business end of a Colt facing in your direction. Jake's own gun came out – firing on the draw. And Clay rocketed backwards.

'You bastard!' Fran screamed. But before she could get her claws on him one of the cowhands behind her, fearful of her getting injured rushing at a drawn gun, grabbed her and swung her out of the way exhorting her to 'Stay out of it, ma'am.'

Jake strutted over to the fallen Clay. 'You all saw that, folks. This mad critter, whoever the hell he is, drew first.' He swung round on the onlookers. 'Ain't that so, *compadres*?'

There were murmured affirmations. Jake sheathed his gun and moved to the door, casually like he was on a Sunday afternoon stroll.

'Well, just you tell that to the law when they turn up.'

Fran struggled free and inspected Clay's wound. It was in his gun arm. 'Chrissakes, somebody fetch a doctor.'

As she comforted him the sheriff arrived and bystanders explained the circumstances. Eventually the lawman knelt beside Fran.

'OK, who was the shootist?'

'An all-round desperado. Wanted for murder, bank heists, you name it.'

He nodded. 'Well he's headed out of town now.' He crossed to the bar. 'I'll take a drink now that I'm here.'

'Aren't you gonna send a posse after him?' Fran shouted after him.

'My jurisdiction ends right at the town limits,' he said without turning round. 'What happens, or has happened, beyond that is somebody else's bag. All the guys here tell me the feller used his gun in self-defence. In that case, it was justifiable; and that's all that counts. If I was you, I'd concentrate on looking after your boyfriend there.'

'He ain't my boyfriend.'

'Well, that's something else I don't want to know about.'

Almost a week later Connie and her sisters turned up at St Bernard. They had been making no headway until the ever-vigilant Connie had spotted a newspaper report of the incident at the town. Neither Jake or Fran had given real names and the name of Clay Morgan meant nothing to her, but there was enough in the description of the incident to arouse her curiosity; and she had played a hunch.

After enquiries, they found Fran tending a wounded Clay in the house of a woman who had kindly offered her premises for the recuperation of the invalid.

'Looks like this is the end of the trail,' Fran said when the family members had brought each other up to date. 'Not much we can do now that Clay is out of action.'

'The hell it's the end of the trail,' Connie said. 'I haven't come this far just to give up now.'

'Well, what can we do?'

'We don't need a man and gun to nail him. We're Shaw women with the family blood running through our veins. Look at all the things our folks went through. They didn't give up when they hit a big hurdle, did they? And we don't.'

She pondered a while. 'Fran, you stay here looking after Clay and Bess. I'm too close on Bridger's trail to let him slip away. Trouble is, I still don't know what the bastard looks like – which is an advantage because it means he doesn't know what I look like. So, Meg, you ride along with me to identify him if we get in range of the bozo. Wear that derby hat and waistcoat that you wore playing the squeezebox. Our Mr Jake shouldn't recognize you in that gear. I didn't for a spell.'

'How we going to find him?'

'We've found him once. We can find him again. Besides, he's going to be off-guard now he thinks Fran and Clay are out of the way. Bet he thinks he's got a charmed life.'

'He works to a plan.' Fran explained. 'Got all his prospective heists mapped out.'

'You get a look at it?' Connie wanted to know.

'Sure. I got a rough idea where he was heading.' She thought about it some more. 'But it might not be helpful. He will have cancelled his plans now.'

'But he's methodical,' Meg said. 'Does he still keep that little book?'

'Yes,' Fran said.

'What book?' Connie asked.

'A little book he keeps a load of notes in,' Meg said. 'All kinds of information that might be useful. Descriptions of towns, whether they got telegraph or not. How many lawmen in town. Stage and train schedules. He might have cancelled his plans, but he's not one to waste anything. I figure he'll use the time going round his planned route and bringing himself up to date on information – all ready for when he restarts operations.' Then the excitement left her voice. 'So we find him, then what?'

Connie lit a cigarette.

'Good job Ma isn't around to see you doing that,' Bess said, pulling a wry face and exaggeratedly wafting away the smell with her hand.

'Bess, sweet soul,' Connie said, her mind elsewhere, 'you don't know half.' She studied the smoke curling upwards in slow spirals. 'We've got to play on his faults. Use them to his disadvantage somehow. You know him, girls. I don't. What are his faults?'

'Vain as a peacock,' Meg said.

'Mean, ornery temper,' came from Fran.

'More than that, he's a greedy bastard,' Bess said in her slow way.

Connie studied the smoke some more. 'That's it,' she said. 'Greed. Gives me an idea.' She opened her saddlebag, rooted through its contents until she found a piece of folded paper. She opened it on the table and studied the scrawls.

The girls gathered around. 'What is it?' Meg asked.

'A useless piece of paper left me by an old-timer,' Constance explained. 'Don't know why I didn't throw it away back in Arrowhead.'

'So what's the idea?' Fran wanted to know.

'Stories of buried loot marked with an X on a treasure map are just about the corniest tales in the West,' the eldest sister mused. 'Nobody pays them much mind. But our Mr Bridger might just fall for it. As long as it's dressed up right.'

'You said it's a useless piece of paper,' Bess said. 'If it's useless I don't see how it can help us.'

'This can't,' Connie said. 'But if we were to prepare another one, one that takes him to a very dangerous place . . .' Her voice trailed off and the others remained silent. They knew she was thinking things through.

'Yes,' she went on after a spell. 'A very dangerous place. But we gotta fix it so he thinks he's getting something valuable. We can't hand it to him on a plate. He would be suspicious – or just dismiss it, like I dismissed the old man's chart. The critter's got to think it's genuine. And then we fix it so he steals it.' She looked around the room. 'Now, I need some ink and paper. Better still – a square of fine deerskin, something like that.'

14

Jake Bridger faced a tableful of sober faces. He had decided he was going to win this hand and it was as though the rest of the players in the game knew it. He duly raked in his winnings and began shuffling the cards.

'Who's the doll?' a red-haired fellow asked as Jake's fingers skimmed the cards across the table.

'Came in on the stage this afternoon,' another said.

'Who is she?' Red persisted.

'Dunno. Passing through. Scuttlebutt is she's a schoolteacher on her way to a new position. Bedding down here at the hotel till the next stage comes through.'

Jake didn't take part in the interchange but he sensed the woman's perfume as she continued past the table. Once he had assessed the cards in his hand he turned to watch her ascend the stairs. He could tell why the guys were interested – she was a looker for sure – then he returned to his cards.

Some ten minutes later he noted her return and watched her order a sarsaparilla at the bar.

As he continued with the game he was aware of her watching the play.

'This looks an amusing way of passing some time,' she said at the conclusion of a hand. Her refined accent had a certain incongruity amid the rough-voiced bullwhackers. 'Can anyone join in?'

Nonplussed, the players looked at her. It was rare to hear such manner of speech – even more to have a woman at the table.

'I don't see any objection,' one said after contemplating the suggestion and glancing around at the other players. 'You can play, ma'am?'

'What's the game called?' she asked.

Stupid female, Jake thought. Doesn't even know what the game is.

'Poker,' the red-headed one said, sweeping in the current pot.

'Well, I've never played it before,' she went on, 'but I'd be eager to learn.'

The red-headed one smiled and shook his head. 'I think not, ma'am. It's only fair to tell you that we're seasoned players and it would be an expensive way for you to learn.'

The cards were dealt again and play resumed with the woman watching intently.

'It looks very much like the game I have seen gentlemen-friends playing,' she said when the hand came to an end. 'You know, with their brandies after dinner. Brag, I think they called it.'

The red-headed one chuckled patronizingly as

he pushed forward the ante for the next hand.

'Yes, ma'am, there are similarities. But brag is a more genteel form of pastime. More suited to, as you say, refined gentlemen in some Eastern club-room.'

The woman watched another deal through to its conclusion. 'It seems to me as I observe here, that the principle of the two games is the same.' She giggled and added, 'Although I must admit I've never played brag either.'

This time no one spoke, just threw knowing glances at each other as they prepared for the next hand. The female was going to become a nuisance if she stood there, chattering and commenting all through the action.

'We're here to play, not jawbone,' one muttered, slapping down his cards and gathering the rest in order to deal.

At the end of the next round, one of the company histrionically threw in his busted flush and stared at the table, his eyes clearly saying goodbye to his money.

'Well, guys,' he said, rising, 'that's cleared me out for the night.' He counted coins from his pocket and clutched them hard. 'I've got enough nickels to buy one more drink and I ain't hazarding them.'

Before anyone could say otherwise the woman took occupancy of his vacated chair and put her purse on the table. She opened it and took out a wad of bills. 'Does anyone object if I take the gentleman's place?'

Around the table, eyes widened as they
surveyed the stack of currency.

'I feel lucky tonight,' she went on. 'I've just won
this money on the roulette-wheel across the
street.' She chuckled 'I've never played that
before. Two hundred dollars I think the man said
when I cashed in my chips. So, gentlemen, I have
the wherewithal to play and I've observed enough
of the way you play this game to have a go. It
could be fun.'

Again no one spoke.

'I'm sure you gentlemen will be courteous
enough to allow a lady to chance her luck again,'
she pressed. 'Is that not so?'

'Listen, ma'am, ' the red-headed one said, a hint
of irritation in his voice, 'put your money away.
That's too much mazuma to lose to a bunch of
strangers. And, believe me, you would lose. Betting
on a ball bouncing on the frets of a roulette-wheel
is one thing; anybody can win. And, judging by
that stack, there ain't no gainsaying Lady Luck
has been smiling on you already tonight. But card
playing is a different matter, ma'am.'

She smiled and patted the pile of sawbucks.
'That's a chance I would be willing to take. Easy
come, easy go, that's my motto. As I said, I do feel
lucky.'

'If the lady insists, let her play,' Jake said,
mesmerized by the green mountain before her. He
was still short of the folding stuff and could
suddenly see his meal-ticket within grabbing
distance. 'I've no objection.'

'Right,' she said, relaxing into her seat, 'if that's settled, will someone be so kind to explain the rules. I've observed enough to know the reckoning is something to do with the ranking of combinations.'

One of the company shrugged. 'On your own head be it, ma'am,' he said, realizing they were not going to shut this woman up until someone had cleared her out of her entrance ticket. There was a general shaking of heads in expression of the unpalatability of allowing in an intruder, especially one of the feminine gender, but there were no vocal objections.

Jake was only too pleased to accede to her request and spent a minute explaining the procedure, ranking of hands and the method of betting.

'You got that, ma'am?' he said when he'd finished.

'I got it, sir,' she said. 'Now, will someone please deal.'

The game proceeded for a while but the woman who had been irritating in her chattering from the sidelines was now equally irritating in her very slow play. She spent inordinate amounts of time contemplating her cards at each deal; then would painstakingly count out her stakes in turn. And watching her deal was akin to watching prairie grass grow.

After a few hands, exasperated players began to make their excuses and leave until there was only Jake, the red-headed man and the woman remaining.

It was then that Jake decided to act. He wanted this baby to himself and he had to squeeze out the redhead. He was a skilled card-sharp and, from that point on in the game whenever it was his deal, he made sure the other fellow picked up duds.

'You were talking about luck, ma'am,' the man said eventually, finding himself repeatedly forced to fold. 'I don't mean any discourtesy but you brung nothing but bad luck to me ever since you put your pretty butt on that seat. Time for me to call it a night.'

From then on, now just the two of them, Jake slipped the woman good cards, prompting her to raise her bets. When they were up to fifty dollars a hand he went in for the kill, giving himself three jacks and a pair to her duff hand. He raised and raised until all her roulette winnings were sitting in the middle of the table together with every dime he'd got.

In his excitement he over-betted and was fifty dollars short come the showdown.

'I'm no judge of these things,' she said. 'I'll accept that ring in lieu of fifty.'

He eased the golden entwined snake from his finger, added it to the pot and laid down his winning combination.

'Full house, ma'am.' Then, to soften the blow, he added, 'Like you said, easy come, easy go.'

'I can't believe it,' she said, wide-eyed. 'Tonight really *is* my night. Easy come, easy *come*.' And she laid down her cards. 'When you explained the rules, you did say four of a kind beat a full house, didn't you? I can't believe it.'

She couldn't believe it? *He* couldn't believe it. *Four kings*.

His eyes narrowed as his gaze moved from the colourful quartet of pasteboards to the innocent-looking features of the woman opposite. Innocent? Like hell. But there was damn all he could do. In front of the gathered audience he couldn't say, *I know you're cheating, woman, because I dealt you nothing more than a couple of aces to keep you interested.*

'Another hand?' she suggested, reaching forward and delicately rendering the centre of the table devoid of currency.

He shook his head. 'I'm clear out of scratch,' he grunted. 'You sure have beginner's *luck*, ma 'am.'

'Oh, what a pity,' she said. 'Just as I was getting the hang of it. Well, thank you for the game. It was very enlightening. And now that I have some understanding of what it is about I look forward to playing again sometime. Poker, you say it's called? I must remember the name.'

Powerless, he watched as she packed the scrip into her bag. *His* scrip. Pasting on one of his best smiles, he lifted his backside off the seat and extended his hand.

'It's been a pleasure, ma'am. A *costly* pleasure, but a pleasure all the same. Jake McCoy at your service.'

McCoy, that's a new one, she thought as she delicately touched his hand.

'Constance Beauregard. The pleasure is mutual, sir. And thank you for your forbearance with a beginner.'

He resumed his seat and watched as she finished her sarsaparilla, then crossed to the bar.

'Drinks all round,' she announced, dropping some bills on the bar. 'Good night, gentlemen.'

And she glided up the stairs.

Jake lay on his bunk unable to sleep. He couldn't get the damn woman out of his mind. Boy, was she a pro. Not only at cards but the way she had suckered them all in. She'd encouraged the impression that she was fresh from some chintz-draped Eastern drawing-room, but the way she had pulled herself four kings out of nowhere – that was the mark of a real fancy-fingerer.

A slicker himself, he'd been suckered by a slicker – and that stuck in his craw. He seethed with rage, his mind dominated by getting back his money – with interest – and maybe getting her up a dark alley and smacking her in the mouth a few times as a bonus. But the more he contemplated the evening's events the more he fought these feelings. Be sensible, boy, he told himself. Cool down, think of the longer term. Immediate satisfactions like slapping her around could wait. The fact was he was in need of a new woman partner. Using a female stooge was the way he worked – he didn't know any other – but up to now he'd always used young dumb chickens. Maybe it was time to get classy.

His imagination worked. Partnering-up with a dame such as this could pave the way to much bigger hauls. With her skill, bearing and panache, together they could pull off some real big scams. The world was full of railroad barons, financiers and the like, ready for plucking. All it needed was brains and a couple of classy operators. Maybe tonight had presented him with the break he had been waiting for. One thing was for sure. He'd have to mask his desire for revenge. He felt confident about getting close to the dame. That was no problem. He'd always been able to charm women. Something about his looks and manner had made the feminine gender putty in his hands all his life – right from the time he was pulling down knickers behind the schoolhouse. But he'd have to be more subtle with this baby. She was mature, clever and shrewd. His fawning would have to be less obvious.

Scarcely had the day begun when he was pulling on his pants. He washed and splashed some cologne around his newly shaved features. By the time he had got down to the street a few townsfolk were going about their business. He strolled along the boardwalk and took occupancy of a chair under an awning opposite the hotel where she was staying. From his vantage point he had a view into the dining-room. He lit a cigarette and watched, looking for signs that the building was waking up. He was looking for the woman coming to have breakfast.

But after a few smokes he was still waiting; then he espied her approaching the hotel along the boardwalk. Huh, some early bird, he mused. He watched her disappear through the doorway, then reappear in the dining-room. She took a seat at a table and ordered breakfast. He waited until she was nearing the end of her meal before he crossed the street and passed through the entrance. Besides the woman there was one other guest dining. Jake sat down at one of the other half a dozen tables and ordered a coffee.

'Morning, ma'am,' he offered when the waiter had disappeared. She reciprocated perfunctorily and continued with her meal. The waiter had just brought his coffee when the remaining diner left the room. Eventually the woman elegantly placed her cutlery on an empty plate.

'May I join you, ma'am?' Jake asked when the waiter had brought her a cup of coffee and cleared the table.

'Certainly.'

'Fine day,' he commented as he sat before her.

She looked out of the window. 'Indeed, a fine day.'

He took a sip of his drink. 'I enjoyed the game last night.'

'Considering its outcome, that is gallant of you to say so.'

He looked back at the door to check they were still alone and asked in a lowered voice. 'Can I speak frankly, ma'am?'

'I don't see why not.'

He retained the smile that was permanently pasted on his face and whispered, 'You're no schoolteacher. And you sure ain't the poop you make yourself out to be.'

'I don't know what you mean.'

'You knew I was rigging the cards when you pulled out those four kings. Because we are kindred spirits, I don't mind admitting my chicanery. But that was real sharp of you, ma'am. I admire your skill.'

There was no change in her expression. 'I still don't know what you are talking about.'

'It took me some time,' he went on, 'before I figured out how you did it.'

No reaction showed in her features.

'Yeah,' he continued. 'Nobody's gonna be concerned – or even notice – if a fumbling beginner drops her hand below the table for a split second. You and I know a card-sharp needs some business to distract attention. All that gauche clumsiness and naïve chatter was a cover – the oldest trick in the book. I sure have to hand it you, ma'am – it was brilliant. I figure you could faro-shuffle or ribbon-spread a deck with the best.'

As he spoke he examined her features, searching for a reaction. But, like that of the Mona Lisa, her half-smile gave nothing away. He persevered. 'None of the knuckleheads round that table knew what was going on. Come on, ma'am, give me some credit. You'd got my number. Only difference was I hadn't got yours till it was too late. We're bunko artists, the pair of us. It takes one to know one.' She still didn't speak. 'We're of a kind,' he continued. 'You mask it well. Although I can't see it behind those beautiful peepers of yours, I can tell we know the same thing.'

'And what is that, pray?'

'That the only voice worth listening to is the voice of money.'

She let out an unhurried 'Mmm'. Then, 'Let us say – just for the sake of discussion, you understand – that you had found yourself being gypped at the table, what would you do about it?'

'All depends.'

'On what?'

'Circumstances. If it was a four-flushing grubliner, he wouldn't get far with my money in his pocket. Now, a lady such as yourself. That could make a difference.'

'What difference?'

'I might make a proposition.'

'Such as?'

'Ma'am, the world is designed for people like you and me to take a cut out of.'

'You may as well go on.'

But at that point the waiter returned to clear the tables and Jake hesitated during the bustle and clatter of cutlery. The lady drained her cup and dabbed her lips with the napkin. 'Why don't we continue this discussion in my room?' she suggested, neatly refolding the cloth and placing it on the table.

On the upstairs landing the lady took a key from her purse, handed it to the man and gave her room number. When they reached it, he opened the door and indicated for her to enter. She remained immobile.

'No, after you.' Following him in she closed the door adroitly behind her with her foot.

He turned and noted her hand was still in her purse. He paused before he spoke.

'That a gun, ma'am?'

'Of course it is. And if you were so astute as to hear the click you are astute enough to know it's cocked. I'm a weak woman behind a closed door with a stranger from whom I have taken a considerable amount of money – which, by the way, is now safely banked. That's why I went out first thing this morning. As you said last evening, I am not a poop. So, sit over there where I can see you and tell me what this proposition of yours is all about.'

'Point is, ma'am, we both know the score. We're in the same line. Together the two of us could really clean up.'

'In what way, specifically?'

'My style has always been to work with a woman. And I ain't been caught yet.'

'What kind of work?'

'Banks, anyplace where's there's money for the taking. See, an innocent-looking man and woman – puts everybody off their guard. Works every time.'

'Bank stick-ups? Oh no.'

'I'm not suggesting crude stick-ups. That's my past. See, I've never been in cahoots with somebody of style like yourself. No, I'm thinking of real big scams. Bigger than hauls from local banks. I got ideas for setting up big-dealing financiers and such.'

She shook her head. 'I appreciate the offer but I always work alone.'

'Two heads are better than one, ma'am,'

'I know. I've been thinking that way myself.'

'Well, if you've got something in mind. I'm your man. We'd make a great team.'

Again the head shook. 'Mr McCoy, I'm afraid the territory is full of you and your kind. I am in search of someone special.'

15

'I'm honoured that you should pass a message that you wanted to see me, ma'am.'

It was the next evening and Jake and Connie were seated in the hotel lobby. 'How can I be of service?' he went on.

'I've been thinking about what you said, Mr McCoy. About two heads being better than one. Can I trust you?'

'Implicitly.'

'Then let me show you something.' She opened her bag and took out the specially prepared map. 'I have travelled a long way and here is my destination. You see here.' She indicated a circle on the map. 'There is a fortune in bills cached in a well at a disused homestead near a place called Monument. See, the location is clearly marked.'

He appraised it warily, his features unmoving. 'How do you know it's genuine?' he said slowly.

'My dear sir, it's genuine, all right. It belonged to my dear late husband.'

'So?'

'As you have already so astutely observed, there's more to me than meets the eye. There was

more to my dear husband too, God bless him. We
were of the same ilk. And he was a good provider.
Amassed a considerable fortune.'

'Doing what?'

She smiled enigmatically. 'Through activities,
shall we say, in which he sailed very close to the
wind. Consequently we lived very well. Big house,
all the trappings. What was left over he stashed
away. This was left to me in his will.'

'A cache of bills? Tucked away just like that in
the middle of nowhere? Wasn't he worried that
somebody might stumble across it?'

'That's the clever part. He fixed up signs warning people to keep away because of Indians. And
who's going to go rummaging about at the bottom
of a disused well, anyhow? It's just sitting there.
So, Mr McCoy, those are the facts of the situation.
I'm on my way there now. Only trouble it's a mite
bleak out there as you can imagine. The fact is, I
now realize I need a partner to see me through
the last stages of my journey. An escort, a man
who can handle himself. Of course, he would be
well paid.'

He nodded. 'Mrs Beauregard, I'm your man.'

'Good. I feel more secure already.' She sighed.
'Now that's fixed up there's no need to rush, and I
am still rather weary from travelling. I'd dearly
like to rest up a spell. So, now everything's fixed
up, let's say we take it easy and commence our
journey in a couple days.'

'Whatever you say, ma'am.'

She tucked the map back into her bag and

extended her hand. 'Fine. Let us shake on it.'

'Yes,' he said. 'And even better, let us drink on it.' He leaned over and clutched her arm to consolidate their new familiarity. 'And none of your sarsaparilla this time.'

'Very well, but not too much. If there's one thing I can't take in any quantity it's alcohol. Goes straight to my head.'

For the rest of the evening she let him ply her with wine. Late on, she feigned drunkenness. 'I must retire,' she said eventually. 'Or I'll fall asleep right here downstairs.'

'Let me escort you to your room.' She staggered exaggeratedly up the stairs. Inside her room she dropped her bag on a chair near the door and collapsed on the bed. She murmured a 'goodnight' and he dutifully left the room.

Half an hour later, while she emitted loud pretend snores, she heard the door being opened. Her grip tightened on the gun levelled right at the position he would be if he approached her reclining figure. She could hear his breathing as he stood considering. There was the sound of guarded rummaging in her bag, then the door closed again; then the soft tread of feet down the hall.

She waited a while, then crossed to the chair. She opened the bag and checked the map had gone. She smiled and locked the door. In the dark she went to the window and opened it. The street was deserted and quiet. When she heard horse's hoofs fading into the distance she returned to her bed and allowed herself to drift off into proper sleep.

Come morning it was with satisfaction that she learned that her Mr McCoy had mysteriously left town.

Jake eased himself down the well. Although he had come equipped with a lantern, extensive searches had revealed nothing.

'Damn bitch,' he growled eventually. His fingers raw with clawing he fell against the wall. 'Looks like she's tricked me. Tricked me *again*. But why? Why send a complete stranger on a fool's errand? I didn't even know the damned woman.'

He returned to his probing and scraping, but an hour later he resigned himself to a wasted effort. He clambered back up towards daylight, cursing all the way. He stopped cursing when he got to the top. He couldn't curse; the first arrow went through his windpipe.

Some months on and many miles away out in the Badrocks, four women and a man were standing around a newly dug hole in a cave, jubilation written large on their faces.

'The dear old codger was right,' Connie said. 'There's enough here to see us all into old age.'

'You still haven't told us who the old feller was,' Meg prompted. 'The one who gave you the map.'

'Just an old friend from way back,' Connie said absently, and continued voicing her ideas. 'I

can see us now – running the biggest ladies'
emporium in Denver.'

She turned to Clay, who had his father's snake
ring back on his finger. His nearly healed arm
hung at his side, while the other was around
Fran. 'There's a job for you too, Clay,' she said.
'We're going to need accounts doing, records keeping – and a man about the place. That's if you
want it.'

'Of course, I want it,' he smiled, pulling Fran
closer to him.

A couple of hours later they reached town and
stashed the money into valises; then returned
their hired horses and pack-asses to the ostlers.
There was half an hour to kill before the Denver
stage came through.

'Come on, girls,' Constance said. 'There's time
for a celebratory drink. You're all old enough to go
in a saloon now.'

'Like we've never been in one before,' Meg
grinned, looking knowingly at her other sisters.

Within a few minutes they were standing at a
bar with raised glasses while puzzled regulars
looked on at the strange bevy of women who had
invaded their watering-hole.

From her bag Constance took out a crumpled
newspaper cutting that she had picked up from
Monument as they had passed through. She
smoothed it out and looked at it. The piece
detailed the death of a stranger, killed by
Indians out on the Grounds. He was unidenti-

fied save for the mention of a missing finger.

She raised her glass. 'To the end of an ornery bastard.'

When that toast was out of the way she raised her glass again. 'And now to a more pleasant toast. To Fran and Clay.'

After that, Clay bought another round and raised his glass. 'And here's to the Shaw sisters.'

With glasses nearly empty, Constance raised her glass yet again. 'One final toast – Happy Christmas.'

'Christmas?' Bess queried. 'It's the middle of June. What do you mean, Connie?'

Their elder sister said nothing.

Just downed her drink, smiled and headed for the door.